Critical Acclaim

Grace of Falling Stars review by Abby Coutinho, *South Shore Review*

Bruce Meyer offers a solution to the uncontrollable complexity of time by presenting places where time does not exist, most notably the writings of oneself and others. In poems such as "Museum of Reading Habits" and "Paragraph" the idea of timelessness is presented with a distinct grace that is reflected in the title of the collection. A level of elegance is sustained as Meyer traverses his way through the most grueling topics while simultaneously creating an inviting environment for the reader to bask in their melancholy and celebrate the inevitable fall from grace we are all forced to face.

The Hours: Stories from a Pandemic review by
Abby Coutinho, *South Shore Review*

Meyer's writing is refreshingly earnest and reflective of how so many people have been feeling for the past year. A particular line from his first story "The Yellow Jack" speaks volumes about the quiet ache that's been sitting in our throats for the past year: "he was a dot on a map one minute, and a place that no longer existed the next." Life's fragility contributes to the instability of our reality, and Meyer convinces the readers that it might be worth it to embrace the unknown and accept our newfound normal.

The stories reveal an underlying facet of the human experience that transcends historical generations; an unprecedented motivation to transform our lowest moments into inspiration to reach the highest peaks of mortality, as sometimes our darkest moments define the most radiant types of pure hope. Reminiscent of John Keats' classic "Ode to Melancholy," Meyer's whimsical writing reminds us that the most joyous sentiments are steeped in the lingering memory of tragedy which fuels us to ponder the dismal moments so we may celebrate and indulge in life's treasures when they come to us. From an accustomed love rejuvenated by music or a decrepit island united by a tight-knit community, Meyer presents a warm essence that bestows the book with both a timely and timeless flare.

Re: *Portraits of Canadian Writers*, PQL, 2016 (National Bestseller)
Review by Meg Nola, *Foreword Reviews*

Portraits of Canadian Writers could be described as an admirable project, but what takes the collection to an exceptional level is Meyer's devotion to and passion for Canada's literary legacy. His impressions of and meetings with these portrait subjects are memorably joyous, quirky, respectful, and poignant by turns, with his ultimate goal being to bring well-deserved recognition to such a diverse group and all "the dreams they put into words."

Farzana Naz Shampa – Introduction to Bangla
edition of Bruce Meyer's Poetry

By the grace of almighty God, my first literary translation work has been published. This Bengali book features various poems of Poet Bruce Meyer, renowned Canadian academic and inaugural Poet laureate City of Barrie , Ontario.

I express my sincere gratitude to Professor Bruce for allowing me to translate his amazing poems as well as for writing an amazing foreword for the book.

Poet Bruce's poetry shines light on the realistic illustrations of Canada's nature, beautiful layouts and positivity from every source of life. I am always touched by his works. Poet Bruce appears in different roles through his poems ~ sometimes as protesting teenager, a nationalist, general worker at the railway station, an affectionate father,a grateful child with a memory of the mother's two active hands or a dreamy teenager.

Through my work, I want to present Canadian literature in my mother tongue - Bengali. Whatever gap exists in this area can be mitigated, among others, through translation works so people of two cultures and countries can learn about each other's through its literary works.

49th Shelf
Re: *Down In the Ground*, Guernica Editions

Dying is not merely the domain of the dead; it is a shared experience. What remains after someone has passed are the memories, that reflections of the past and those who have passed, and the challenges everyone faces in the wake of loss. *Down in the Ground* is a collection of short, flash fiction stories that examine the ways in which individuals deal with grief and loss, not as morbid reactions but as attempts to understand what they are experiencing. From the cradle to the grave, *Down in the Ground* is a study in the complex creativity we use to address grief and to challenge death so that life can triumph.

Sachi Nag, Interview in *The Artisinal Writer* of *Toast Soldiers*

What is your definition of a successful piece of writing? Who decides that?

Do not confuse success with perception of completeness. Success is for someone else to decide. A writer should never pat themselves on the back and say "I'm a success" because that sort of perception is always short-lived. I have watched hundreds of writers come and go through my career. They had their moments and then were forgotten. The American poet Jack Gilbert in his poem "The Abnormal Is Not Courage" ends with the great line that courage is "The normal excellence of long accomplishment." A writer is only as good as his or her current work and bringing that work to life means pouring their soul into it. But it is not for the writer to say what is successful or not successful. The writer is only permitted to say "that works" and if it doesn't to use his or her skill to fix the problems. A successful piece of writing by someone else goes "Ping!" and that is when all the parts come together and the memory of the piece doesn't leave my mind.

The Miramichi Reader, Interview with Bruce Meyer,
re: *Toast Soldiers* by James M. Fisher

Can you talk about the title? What inspired it?

Meyer: As I mentioned, the title was inspired by brunch. What I haven't told anyone is that I had a set of 78 rpm recordings by the Canadian comic (who lived and worked in England in the Thirties) Stanley Maxted, and his gem was A.A. Milne's "The King's Breakfast," which he set to music. The Milne poem is about hierarchies, ranks. It should be played in every office in Canada. "The King asked the Queen / And the Queen asked the Dairymaid / Could I have a little bit of butter for my bread…" The cow eventually gets the message but answers "Many people nowadays prefer marmalade instead." The poem is the classic statement on administrivia. My point is that inspiration, even in its most profound sense, does not come from profound places or ideas. The challenge is for the writer to drill down into a fragment of the commonplace and make it into something more than anyone could have foreseen with the source. Isn't that what resides at the core of invention?

What was the most difficult story to complete in *Toast Soldiers*?

Part of me wants to say all of them. Stories are easy to begin but the real work resides in finishing them. The hardest one to complete was likely "Oglevie," because the character is so beaten down by life and the art of boxing. That story was inspired by Tolstoy's remark that there are really only two stories (and I had the feeling he was thinking of Homer's Odyssey which is the underpinning story in "Oglevie"). A stranger leaves town. A stranger returns. I kept asking myself if justice in an unkind, hostile universe, would be possible, and if even an inkling of it is possible, what would that justice (or call it mercy if you wish) look like? With the other stories, I can see then end the moment I thought of the beginning, and I knew what I had to do to reach the finale. Not so with "Oglevie." In the end, I gave him a shred of the mercy he deserved. I had been inspired by the line from Richard Hugo's poem, "Degrees of Grey in Phillpsburg" where Hugo says the misery won't let up "until the town inside you dies." The question I was wrestling with was "how does one find life and redemption in that town inside the protagonist when it is apparent to all the town has died?" Endings are never a problem for me, though getting to them can be a test of my wits.

Interview with Bruce Meyer, Re: *Toast Soldiers*,
by Evelyn Maguire, *South Shore Review*

Meyer's prose, surprising and clever, runs from whimsical: "Cheese explains so much about the type of person who ought to be murdered" (113), to downright unsettling: "The noises in the forest had bodies and a body is always hungry" (41). Each story operates from its own world, in which the rules of morality tumble and shift in delightful mystery. The recurring theme of the absurdity inherently found within war is reminiscent of Vonnegut — there can be no higher compliment — but there is no mistaking Meyer's prose for anything but his own.

Sweet Things

Sweet Things

Flashes in the Dark

Bruce Meyer

Library and Archives Canada Cataloguing in Publication

Title: Sweet things : flashes in the dark / Bruce Meyer.

Names: Meyer, Bruce, 1957- author.

Description: Short stories.

Identifiers: Canadiana (print) 2022024300X
Canadiana (ebook) 20220243026

ISBN 9781771616560 (softcover) ISBN 9781771616577 (PDF)
ISBN 9781771616584 (EPUB) ISBN 9781771616591 (Kindle)

Classifi c ation: LCC PS8576.E93 S94 2022
DDC C813/.54—dc23

Published by Mosaic Press, Oakville, Ontario, Canada, 2022.

MOSAIC PRESS, Publishers
www.Mosaic-Press.com
Copyright © Bruce Meyer, 2022

Printed and bound in Canada.

 Funded by the Government of Canada
Financé par le gouvernement du Canada

MOSAIC PRESS
1252 Speers Road, Units 1 & 2, Oakville, Ontario, L6L 5N9
(905) 825-2130 • info@mosaic-press.com • www.mosaic-press.com

Contents

CONTENTS

Not knowing is the sweetest life.

Sophocles

In order for the light to shine so brightly the darkness
must be present.

Francis Bacon

Wheel

I am no longer afraid of heights. When I was young, the idea of riding skyward on a Ferris wheel terrified me. My grandmother kept coaxing me to ride with her. She loved roller coasters, too.

"When we get up to the top we can see everything," she said.

Eventually, when I was ten I relented and went on the wheel with her. As we waited at the top for the lower buckets to load, she began to rock our seat back and forth. I wanted to be sick.

By the next summer, she was dying. We watched *The Ed Sullivan Show* on a tv in the ward lounge. Pearl Bailey was singing, "That's Life," about being shot down in April and back on top in June. My grandmother shouted out, "Oh sing it, Pearl!" I'd never heard her that enthusiastic about a song.

After she died, I struggled to keep up with my studies. I suffered a very dark period. My attempts at finding work were a disaster. I began a position in a bookstore, but my cash float was off by ten cents one day. I must have miscounted someone's change. I was accused of stealing and released at the end of the day.

I managed to get to graduate school on the inheritance from my grandmother and studied Medieval literature, not just Chaucer, but his contemporaries – Hoccleve and Gower – and determined to immerse myself in their world.

I took a train one summer morning from London to Rochester in Kent. London was snarled with a state funeral. The only person in Rochester Cathedral was an elderly woman mopping the nave. I asked if the church was open.

At first, she said "No," then looking me up and down decided I was not the sort who might do damage to the place. I had a camera around my neck and a notebook in my hand.

"Stay as long as you wish," she said, "just close the door behind you when you leave." She said she was off to see the funeral and disappeared through a small door on the south aisle. A moment later, she returned and handed me an annotated floor plan.

There is no feeling like having a gothic cathedral all to oneself. Sound, light, air soar upwards. The alabaster tomb of a Medieval bishop glowed in a column of light. His praying hands lit up like angels. In the silent enormity of the church, I wanted to say the word "Amen," but refrained for fear I would break the spell of the sanctuary. Birds were arguing in the eaves. The rest was stillness.

I ascended the steps of the chancel and stood looking the length of the rows, each seat shoulder to shoulder with the next in a congregation of ghosts. I was about to turn away and walk down into the nave when I saw a patch of column that wasn't whitewashed on one of the pillars facing me.

Beneath the layers of Puritan erasure was a Medieval wall painting. A queen was standing beside a Ferris wheel. I studied her face. She bore an uncanny resemblance to my grandmother, or perhaps I just wanted to see her likeness there because I promised her that someday I would ride a Ferris wheel with her and not be afraid.

In ascending buckets of the wheel, kings were donning their crowns. On the descending side, monarchs were tumbling from their seats, their diadems falling from their heads as they fought to grasp at an illusion. I sat down on the chancel steps and read the guide sheet. The painting depicted a passage from Boethius' *Consolation of Philosophy*. As it faced the altar, it was meant to instill in the priests, even at the moment of their greatest power, the humility that says all success and worldly worth are but rumors. I wanted to shout out, "Oh sing it Pearl!" because at last, I understood the life my grandmother had led. Two wars, the Great Depression, the years of scraping by, days and nights of hardship – all they had given her was the right to let go and fling her arms in the air as the coaster cars roared downward.

A bookstore near the station had reopened after the funeral and I found a copy of Boethius. In his despair, as he languished in a Roman prison, he argued that all fortune is an illusion. One day can be good, the next awful. I thought about my grandmother asking me to join her on the wheel if only so we could reach the top and she could rock the bucket until I was not afraid. And had I relented and risen with her as far as we could go, the view would have been stunning.

The Langlois Bridge
(Longlisted Strand International Fiction Contest)

I am seated beside a blond woman on the bank of the Bouc Canal outside Arles, the town Van Gogh painted at the height of his career. The narrow lift bridge destroyed by the retreating Germans in 1944 is still intact. The colors in the dream are more vivid than if I was inside a rainbow. I recall holding the woman in my arms when we woke that morning.

What frightens me is the feeling I get as we pass a bottle of wine back and forth and talk about Vincent's letters, the passion he exuded as he struggled to see this world from the vantage of another. He wasn't mad. He was simply somewhere else and watching our madness from far away. What frightens me is that I don't know who you are. Are you someone I knew in another life? Is the painting merely the depiction of a bridge or is it a mask:

There are likely more realms of existence – more things in Heaven and Earth than are dreamt of in my philosophy – that we cannot see or know. The beauty of the moment is real to me. You are real to me, and what frightens me is that I lost you. Happiness, success, wealth, joy, love are all contingent on where one wakes and all are illusions, veils life puts on the keep us from seeing the details of even our own lives.

From what I remember as we lounge on the banks of that canal on a summer afternoon and glance at the bridge that existed years before I was born into my current life, I told you I was leaving. I hated my job and hadn't had a vacation in seven years.

I was tired just as I am tired in my current life. The more things change, the more they stay the same. I needed to find something.

"Let me come with you," you said. "We'll make an adventure from being vagabonds."

That is how I lost you. You came with me. I was selfish. I needed you and now I cannot even recall your name – just your hair and your face and the way you brushed the strands from your forehead in the spring breeze. Were we so close to the end of the times we knew we couldn't see how badly the world would fall apart? A war? Were you killed in the war, perhaps fleeing from it, or a victim of your confidence as you attempted to ride out things too terrible to think about even if I could remember?

Early March is a lousy time to see France. The sky is silver, grey when it is not raining. But I wanted to write and tell you I made it to Arles. The colors were missing. I walked along the canal but I did not find what I was looking for, and I photographed the new bridge across the Bouc Canal but erased the images from my camera.

Later, if I sort out more than I can convey in my words, I will describe the famous scene Van Gogh painted when it is devoid of hope – that moment after the sun goes behind a cloud and a shadow sucks the life out of the sky.

You bought two postcards – one of the bridge as it was before the war and the other of Van Gogh's painting, or one of his paintings of the Langlois Bridge because he did several canvases and each shows something slightly different than the others. You held them up to compare the souvenirs to reality. There are so many realities in what I see that I cannot begin to separate one from the other.

Perhaps I am recalling a postcard that tumbled from an old book my grandmother owned and you are an invention, someone with whom I would have loved to have seen it. Perhaps I simply stepped into a Van Gogh canvas in a museum and I am only now learning how to squeeze through the frame and slip into a far less interesting world that is just as wrought with troubles and fears as the world beyond our field of vision that afternoon by the canal.

This world is attempting to be beautiful but it is disappointing to those who see it as more than it is yet we live with it, refuse to ask what it could be, and accept it as it is in the belief it is the only world we have. I think the blond woman said that to me before she died too young to explore all the other realms our minds can go.

After the canal passes through the narrows of the old Langlois Bridge, it flows out of sight. Van Gogh's studies of the scene question what lies beyond his vantage. The scenes are keyhole studies. There is so much beyond the stone abutments we are not permitted to see. What would happen if we could?

I cannot go to sleep because I have glimpsed a fragment beyond the canvas. I cannot bear to live the moment I am told she has died. When the dream repeats, she continues to die again and again on a rainy afternoon when all the colors have been sucked from the bright world where we lay on the bank of the canal. This world, grey and rainy and chilled in the March wind, is my reminder of the loss I return to in my sleep. For that reason, I close my eyes.

When a painter applies his oils to a canvas he is not merely depicting what he sees nor is he even commenting on what he feels he must show the world: he is covering a void. A painting says there has to be something instead of nothing. When I close my eyes I see nothing at first. That moment is frightening in its own right. Then my mind begins to paint a scene. A bottle of red is propped on the grass between us. Her jacket is a blue and yellow plaid. The waters do not merely sparkle. The canal is a fountain of color. Van Gogh painted the Langlois Bridge from at least five different views and each time the result was the same. We are permitted a glimpse of something far away, but for the most part, the future, or the past, or some other existence is always hidden.

If the rain stops, I will go for a walk along a back road leading out of town to the fields that are waiting to discover life again. If I am lucky and the sky has cleared, the stars will be pinwheels spinning out of control as if trying to break the glass wall between their Heaven and where they desire to be. I will gaze up at their lights as if each wears its own small halo as the moon does on a spring night, and I will see you in their glow and take your hand.

6

Cuba (Retreat West Fiction Prize)

The smell of Cuba is beautiful. Every place has its own smell. London, for example, has a different smell than it used to have. It was unmistakable as you stepped off an airplane and lined up in the Customs and Immigration Hall at Heathrow. London had the aroma of beer, heavy lubricating grease like the kind they use on escalators, and diesel exhaust from cabs. It doesn't smell the same now. It has changed.

I would wait to inhale New York until I got down around 11th Street in Tribeca before it got to be trendy. New York smelled of saltwater, dank basements, car exhaust, and unfiltered cigarettes. Chicago always had a note of feed grain and animal offal. Austin smelled of dust and heat. Heat has a smell. It is dry. You feel as if the inside of your nose is slowly being cooked, and beer, though not English real ale as I detected in London. I can close my eyes and you can put me on a plane and when I land I can tell you where I am.

Havana is my favorite. It smells of the car exhaust I knew from my childhood before emission controls became standard in North America. Rum, a sweet note hiding in the background, but hard to detect. And cigars. Cigars everywhere. That's where I developed my love of what my friends call the most disgusting habit in the world. Cohibas. Cohibas and liquor. I can almost imagine I am in Cuba when I open a bottle of Jack Daniels. There's smoke in there somewhere, which is why I have gone to great lengths to recreate the smell of Cuba. I mustn't forget the note of ocean salt. That's there, too.

My wife left me because I said she smelled like Quebec City, like stone that is cold even in late spring. My dog gets wet in the rain. She's stonily metallic, and sometimes I smell my wife on her, not as she was but as she became. A garrison city. The cold hard smell of a clear day when you look east along the St. Lawrence and you see all the way down to where freshwater meets the sea. But you don't smell fresh water in Quebec City. Everything smells like my wife when she said we were over

I told her she was the stony silence on the seaway, as Leonard Cohen called it. It is the smell of a worn-out relationship, the personal ramparts meant to keep invaders at bay.

That's why I smoke cigars and drink heavy black rum. I want to remember Cuba. I want to smell the saltwater on her skin, a Cohiba between my fingers as she lay down glistening beside me. The oddly out-of-place aroma of coconut suntan lotion after it is salted by the sea.

I want to tell myself I haven't forgotten what love is because I can still smell it, though each reminder is slowly killing me.

The Riverside

The Riverside was nowhere near a river, but Betty needed to get off the road for the night. Her toddler was cranky and had cried himself to sleep in the backseat. The police might be on the lookout for them. She needed a place to lay low, at least for the night. Betty didn't care if the hotel was named for the dark side of the moon.

Mother and son had fled. She had only her grocery money. Jim had been a monster. His drinking had gotten worse and Betty couldn't stand the beatings any longer. Her town should have had a battered women's shelter, but that had been shut down, a victim of a budget shortfall, when Jim's uncle became Mayor. The official excuse stated the town was a Christian community and wives had a duty to obey their husbands.

In her sudden departure, she only had time to grab a box of Cheerios for Benny and scoop up his favorite bear from the floor of his playpen. As she drove away, Betty looked in the rearview mirror and realized she was leaving both the town and her marriage behind. Good riddance to the whole mess.

The Riverside looked safe enough for the night. The motel had a brightly lit sign, though behind the neon lettering of red and blue, the teal paint of the rusting mounting board was peeling. The flowing script, that reminded her of the penmanship on the Declaration of Independence, was antique and out of place with the realities of the world she knew; yet there were enough cars parked outside the rooms with toys in the back seats to give her some assurance the place was not a no-tell-motel. To reinforce her hopes that there were families in those rooms, blue glows and corny laugh tracks from sitcoms echoed across the parking lot as she pulled up in front of the office.

Room 18 wasn't expensive, but it would cost almost every cent she had with her. The clerk barely looked up from the paperwork he handed her.

"I'll need you to pay upfront. Some people walk away. I know you won't, but upfront will be fine. I'll need your driver's license as proof of identity…"

"You won't tell anyone I'm here, will you?"

The clerk could see the bruise on her left temple and shook his head, "no."

"You'll be safe here. The information is for the state and I won't hand it out to authorities unless something dire happens."

Betty didn't know what he meant by dire. Everything was dire. Her life was dire. The car was running low on gas and that was dire. Benny was asleep but when he was awake he was frightened. "The room will take almost all our cash. I'm afraid to use an ATM in case it is tracked."

"Are you on the run?"

"My husband. He beat me this evening. He was drunk. I ran when he threatened my son. I need to know where to go."

"Have you and your child had supper? My wife and I see so many of you ladies on the run. We have some dinner left. Casserole. Not much but tasty. Madge? Can we get a plate out here?"

He looked at Betty and took a twenty off the top of the cash she had given him and slid it across the counter to her. "You'll need this tomorrow once you're clear. My wife has a list of out-of-state shelters. Madge appeared. He gave a flick of his head toward Betty. Madge understood. She returned with a paper plate covered in tinfoil and passed it to Betty.

"We have a pool," he said. "Just in case you want to go for a swim."

"I didn't bring a suit. My son and I — all we have are the clothes on our backs. I may need to make a phone call in the morning. My folks don't know I've finally run from my husband."

"Don't worry about it," he said. "We see so many like you here."

He told Betty his wife could look after Benny in the morning while she made the call.

Her parents had begged Betty not to marry Jim and they hadn't spoken to her since the night she ran off with the man she thought would be the answer to her dreams. Now, she would have to face them, defeated and broken, and they would register disappointment, a letdown at seeing their daughter in such shape. Perhaps they would be happy to see their grandson for the first time. But if they said Benny was the image of Jim

Betty parked outside the door to Room 18. She wondered if she could trust the clerk. Trust was hard to come by. Trust was supposed to be the foundation of matrimony, yet the minute she turned her back on Jim he was sitting at the bar in the bowling alley drinking himself into a rage. A friend had seen him get into the backseat of an expensive SUV with a tall, blonde-haired woman.

"Why can't you be like other girls?" he'd screamed as he threw the dinner she had saved for him against the wall. The pasta stuck. Benny woke up and began crying. To diffuse the situation, in one of his dire moments, she had pointed to the linguini and said, "Look! It is well cooked!" but Jim didn't get the joke and pummeled her. She had thought about running away that night, but she had married her man for better or worse and the blows to her head, the punches to her gut, and the kicks to her kidneys as she writhed on the floor only made things worse.

Room 18 would be different. It would protect them, if only for one night, and then she would have to seek mercy from the world, though she wondered if mercy still existed.

She lifted Benny from his car seat and opened the room door. All motels smell the same, though this one was less musty, less scented toward the carpet powder maids sprinkle on the broadloom as they vacuum to erase the presence of those who have moved on. A faint odor of cigarettes lingered in the air along with a hint of bourbon, and Betty felt the room had not entirely been a place of transience or sadness. Maybe someone had celebrated in Room 18. There was a table and two chairs in the window and two double beds. She pulled back the bedspread on the double bed farthest from the door. She was worried that if Jim burst in he'd snatch his son and do God-knows-what. Room 18 had to be a defendable position.

After settling her son, Betty sat down beside the front window of the room and watched the pool. In the dark, the pool lights glowed with shimmering reflections that twisted as ripples played along the aqua walls. Betty wondered if the boy on the diving board whose mother wouldn't look up from her book was what she and Benny would become.

The boy called to his mother.

She nodded.

He begged her to watch.

She muttered something and the boy replied that this time he wouldn't splash her. Then the woman closed the covers of the novel, stood up with her legs straddling the plastic-webbed recliner. "Well?" she said.

The boy fell forward as if he were a board or a toppled tree or someone had just put a bullet through him, and he was playing dead. He splashed his mother with the spray. His rippled image frog-legged through the luminous depths to the shallow end. When he emerged, shaking silver droplets from his head, his mother was already standing above him with a towel held by its corners.

"I might have known," the mother said to her son.

"I told you," he replied. "I'm falling for you."

The woman shook her head and wrapped the boy in the towel and rubbed his back as he climbed over the splash trough and the gunnel where someone had painted the words "SHALLOW END NO DIVING."

"You're full of malarkey," the woman said, tousling her son's wet hair.

"Look at me! I'll fall right here."

"No, you don't. You'll hit your head on the bottom. Save it for the deep end and you can fall all you want."

The boy crossed his arms and pretended to tip. "Falling for you. Falling now."

"That's because we're all we've got and if we keep moving we'll be fine," she said as she opened the gate the pool's low fence after tucking her novel under her arm. Her other arm was draped around her son. She didn't let him go. Betty understood why.

The boy tiptoed across the parking lot as if the pebbles in the asphalt were pricking the soles of his feet.

Would that be the future for Benny and her? Would she spend the next eight or even ten years running from her abusive marriage?

One night when Betty thought Jim was sober, he got out his guitar and asked her to sing with him, just as she had when they were first together. Jim had a lovely voice. He could play not badly.

He said, "Betty sing for me. I need a song from you."

They had once talked about moving to Nashville and breaking into the country scene.

But a song would not come to mind no matter how hard she tried. He beat her so hard she thought he had cracked her jaw.

She wondered where the woman from the pool and her diving comedian was going, and whether they, too, had nighttime drives down long, tree-covered back roads separated from farms by stagnant ditches, or through empty streets of small towns that had seen better days and loomed out of the darkness like a labyrinth from which she and Benny could not emerge. Was there a way out for them?

She could leave the state but that would be a crime. Jim would win.

Betty closed the drapes, leaving a narrow gap between the panels so the night air could flow into the room and cool the place down. Benny shuffled in the bed and kicked the blanket aside. Maybe he was dreaming of his father. Although he had only just turned two, Benny was almost too big for the playpen she left behind, but her child considered the mesh sides as a fence between himself and his father. The first complete sentence her son spoke was "No, Daddy. Don't hit Mommy."

She could not get out of her head the way her son's tears flowed down his cheeks as she picked him up and ran for the door. The child's tears coursed in delicate rivulets down his face as his eyes had become a watercourse with nowhere to go and no means of holding back the flood. And as she thought of the river that was heaven-knows-where for which the motel was named, she wanted to sit down on its banks and remembered what she left behind.

When she woke before dawn hours later, the flashing blue lights of police cruisers were blocking the entrance and exit to the parking lot. Betty peered through a crack in the drapes. She could see the faces of other nervous women just like herself staring in terror at the troopers in their Smokey-the-Bear hats with guns holstered on their hips. The hotel clerk was tossed up against the outside doorframe of his office. The man nodded. Madge was screaming, "No! No!"

And as the troopers moved toward her wing of the motel, some with their guns drawn and others with flashlights shining into the darkened rooms, Betty was frozen with fear, uncertain if the men in their uniforms had come for her or the mother of the boy who had already died a thousand deaths at the deep ends of a thousand motel pools.

The Paulsens

Mrs. Paulsen wore a housecoat all day and sat smoking at her kitchen table. She spoke in a cackling, raspy voice, and blamed Jane for ruining her stellar career as a radio singer though she had retired twenty years before Jane's birth. Mrs. Paulsen was an invalid. She suffered, she said, from a bad heart and hadn't long to live.

Jane's father was different. He was an outdoorsman, a government geographer who spent long periods away, but always returned to dote on his daughter. On Saturdays, he did woodworking in his garage and would give Jane and me pointers about angles and joints. He called me Sport. Jane was his Sparkle. His jokes were hilarious.

On rainy days we weren't permitted to play spies inside Jane's house. Her mother would tell me I was unkempt if a shoelace was not neatly tied or my shirttail was hanging out. Peering around corners was uncouth.

As Jane's only friend, I was invited to a restaurant for her eleventh birthday. Her mother scolded me for the way I held my knife. Mr. Paulsen wanted desert. His wife said, "Not for children."

The movie was *Gigi* and told the story of a girl whose aunt reminded me of Jane's mother. We had to sit in the loges so Mrs. Paulsen could smoke. Half an hour into the film, the smoke nauseated me. Mr. Paulsen escorted me to the washroom.

"I think I'd better take the boy home," he said to his wife

"Useless bastard," she replied.

Mrs. Paulsen grabbed Jane by the wrist.

Jane cried.

All the way home, her mother chastised me for not coming from a sophisticated family where smoking was a sign of class.

When Jane graduated to junior high school, we drifted apart. I don't think she forgave me for her birthday.

A year after Jane ran away, I woke one Sunday to an ambulance's flashing lights at the Paulsen's. I was certain Mrs. Paulsen had finally died, but when I knocked on their door to offer my condolences to Mr. Paulsen, Mrs. Paulsen answered with tears in her eyes. She said nothing then lit a cigarette.

Vikings

When my wife hung up the phone she said, "That was your cousin Claudia."

"What does she want," I asked.

" She doesn't want to be a Viking."

"There are worse things," I said.

"That's what I told her."

"What's wrong with being a Viking? Some people spend their entire lives being Vikings. It works for them, especially when they're with other Vikings."

"She asked me to ask you to do a DNA test."

"Is she paying for it?"

"She didn't say," my wife said. "

"I don't want my DNA floating around. It could be used for anything."

"She thought she was Scottish. She had the kilt custom-made in the clan tartan with a sporran but the pipe band she joined is insisting she prove she's entirely Scottish – not Irish, not English, not even Welsh. She has to be one hundred percent Scottish or they won't let her in."

"That's ridiculous," I said. "The Scots never struck me as being into hegemony. I don't think they care about that stuff."

"She's in South Carolina and the pipe band is organized by some guy who insists everyone should be pure Scottish."

"You don't have to be Scottish to play the bagpipes. They're played all over the world. The Irish play bagpipes. You know – 'O Danny Boy, the pipes, the pipes are calling?' People play

17

them from the Andes to the Pyrenees and the Urals, especially on mountains where they're less likely to hurt anyone. Lebanon, Yemen, Pakistan. Heck, even the Romans. I saw a Medieval illumination of a pig playing them."

"I told her that but she's inconsolable. The band made her take a DNA test and it came back Viking. Many Scottish people, especially in the north, have Viking ancestry. She wants you to do the test."

" Gunn's a Viking name. Our ancestors left Scotland. They couldn't stand the squeal. If pipes are badly played they aren't friendly. Did you tell her I'm learning recorder? You don't need a blood test for a recorder. You just need to be far away from everyone."

"She's calling back."

I sighed. Maybe I should play Claudia the recorder over the phone.

Claudia reiterated the plea my wife endured. I stopped my cousin mid-sentence.

"If people want to get together and make horrible noises, who they are shouldn't enter into it. Hire yourself out as a lease breaker."

"I need to be Scottish. I don't want to be a Viking," Claudia wept.

"Oscar Wilde said: Be yourself. Everyone else is taken."

"Vikings don't have marching bands," she whimpered.

"They have marauding bands," I replied. "I was thinking of going pillaging this evening. If we lived nearer you could join me. Bring your own torch."

Claudia slammed the receiver. I hadn't taken her seriously, but as the dial tone trumpeted in my ear I was certain I heard the sound of gulls and cold grey waves, and I imagined sailing off the horizon at the end of the world.

Nessun Dorma

When Melanie was ten she saw an art deco poster for *Turandot* in a shop window and knew she destined was to play the princess.

Her grandmother Cho owned a scratchy 78 of the opera. The old woman played the discs in the misplaced belief the narrative was Chinese. Puccini's story, alas, was a European knock-off.

There weren't many parts in opera for Chinese sopranos. *Madame Butterfly* was out of the question. She had to play Turandot. *Turandot* is a rarity in that it features not just one but two Chinese sopranos. The role gave her hope she would meet her own Prince Calaf.

Melanie and Hua were married while performing *The Pearl Fishers* in Amsterdam. An Artistic Director had the bright idea to cast the son of a real pearl fisher, albeit a Vietnamese one, in the role of the Sri Lankan diver.

The night before Melanie's London debut, Hua went missing.

The empty space in their bed was all he harder to bear when he appeared for rehearsal, clutched his chest, and dropped.

She glared at him as he sang the opening bars of "Nessun Dorma."

The performance was canceled. Melanie and Hua, opera's new power couple were unavailable. Enraged her breakthrough had been thwarted, she grabbed her husband his hospital gown and shrieked, "Do you know who you've screwed with? If I find out I'll torture her to death."

Hua begged to sleep.

"No," she shouted. "Not until I have my answer."

The Other Side of the World

After my father showed me how the Earth worked I wasn't afraid of fire. I respected it because I knew what power it held and how it changes not only landscapes but people's perceptions. I have learned how fire walks through the bush, how fast it travels as if it is in searching of something to satisfy its hunger. Fire hunts. It is startled when it meets another fire and changes direction, sometimes, rather than join hands with it. Fire is what we see in the sky first thing in the morning and at the end of the day.

He gave me a globe for my fifth birthday and on it, each country was a different color with the major cities, mostly the political capitals, written in tiny letters. The pinkish-red countries, for instance, had once belonged to the British Empire but he explained those countries didn't anymore because they found their independence. Independence meant a country retained the same color on the map but the color no longer mattered. The French nations were mint green and most of Africa had not sorted itself out yet so there were vast areas known as French West Africa. I asked him if the French were afraid of independence and he answered, "Yes," because there was still a war going on in Algeria.

The way the world worked had to do with a flashlight. Flashlights are useful because they help us discover things in the dark such as the other side of the world. My father turned off the light in my room. The bulb with its batteries seated like bobsledders behind the contact point provided just enough light to imitate the sun. When half the world was bright, that portion of the Earth was in the daytime. The parts that were hidden in darkness were night. The earth was spinning and because it turned somewhere in the world the sun was setting and boys my age were getting ready to hear bedtime stories or science explanations from their fathers before falling asleep. Somewhere else, a day was always beginning. "It never ends," he said, and I asked him if Jesus knew this because he kept saying, "World without end, Amen." My father nodded.

After my father had turned off the light I lay in the darkness and thought about daylight on the other side of the world. I imagined a boy my age being called to get dressed and come and eat his breakfast because otherwise he'd be late for school and wouldn't learn new words that day or be able to color maps of the world green and pinkish red. But in the dark, I could also imagine what the world might be like if it stopped turning. The sun would shine so brightly on the forests it would act like the magnifying glass my father held over a piece of newsprint to show me how the sun's rays, if focused, could set fire to the point where the beam fell like a tiny star. I was also told not to hold a magnifying glass over ants or bugs because they would burn to death.

My teacher had told us all a story about how the sun was pulled by a chariot through the sky. Each day, well before dawn, Apollo who was in charge of light would get into his cart and his horses would race across the sky until they exhausted themselves in the west and night came.

One day his son got to the chariot before him and took a joy ride across the sky except that he did not know how to handle the sun. He almost set the Earth on fire, the people below, writhing like tiny ants in the intense heat and beam of light, were terrified they might burn to death beneath the blanket of even the most protective cloud. I told the teacher she was wrong.

I told her the sun was a flashlight and it was too far away to set fire to the world unless someone had a giant magnifying glass and treated us like ants. She made me stand in a corner with my face to the wall for the last hour of the afternoon.

Burning up was the worst possible thing I could imagine. Most of the kids in m class were afraid of monsters – some wouldn't say so though I knew they were – and they would accidentally admit they had met huge fanged beasts in their bad dreams.

I never had bad dreams about monsters or the Earth catching fire. All I had to do to prove my father right and the teacher wrong was to go out at recess on a sunny afternoon and point my face to the sun.

My eyes would go blind from staring into the bright light. When I came inside, the classroom would appear dark as night until my eyes adjusted. The heat of the sun on my face would turn my skin the color of the former British Empire on my globe, and I would sneeze uncontrollably because my aunts and uncles said they sneezed if they were out in the sun.

The teacher summoned me the next day and told me I had to agree with her version of the truth. The story made no sense. The sun was not a chariot. I had examined it long and hard. There were no wheels. The light in the sky, my father said, came from a ball of fire, from the nuclear explosions like bombs they were testing in the desert. A single sunbeam, he said, could wipe a city off the map. I wasn't sure who I should believe. Sunbeams were small. They drifted across our living room on winter afternoons although my mother said they were just particles of dust lit up by the light through the window. I stood by my father's version of events. The teacher sent me back to the corner for another afternoon. She said she would punish me until I apologized for saying she was wrong.

That is when I got the idea of smuggling the magnifying glass to school. The classroom had large windows that ran from the heating registers to the ceiling. The curtains had been taken down because, the teacher said, the sun had eaten holes in them. I didn't believe her. Maybe it was the horses that ate the curtains. My mother said she'd seen old plow horses munch on just about anything. During recess, I wasn't permitted to go outside because I was being punished.

I went to the cloakroom and took the magnifying glass from my coat pocket, stopping in front of a mirror the girls used to make sure their hair was tucked into their caps before they left for home. My eye appeared huge. I loved that. The giant eyeball said, "I can see everything you are up to!" The teacher's desk was beside the window. The afternoon was clear and bright. I held the glass over the papers on her desk and a thin, twisting whiff of smoke curled upwards from her notes. I stepped back and put the glass between my shirt and my undershirt and went back to the corner with my face pointing inward to the angle.

Within minutes, just as the other kids were returning from recess, the fire alarm sounded. The teacher ordered the students to turn around as fast as they could and gather at a safe distance in the play area outside. She hadn't even noticed I was left behind in my corner.

Soon, the halls were empty. The firemen had not arrived yet. The hatch to the school's flat roof was open because the janitors had been doing work up there all day with a tar box that melted the black asphalt over an open flame. The tar box was directly above my kindergarten classroom, and the fire below had already punched a hole in the roof through which flames were licking.

I found myself looking down on the students. Some were crying. The teachers were trying to push them farther and farther back from the school walls. I crouched down and hit behind a large duct where I thought I wouldn't be seen. My teacher was counting heads. She turned around, looked back at the classroom door, and realized I was still somewhere inside, perhaps frightened by the sound of the fire truck that pulled up to the school like a red chariot. She walked backward, still facing her students, toward the door.

That is when she reminded me of an ant and when the sun flowed through my magnifying glass and focused on the back of her neck in one small precise spot, I imagined that I had the reins of the chariot. My father would be angry, though when she slapped the spot on her neck and looked up. I was careful not to be seen. I crawled across the pebbled roof and down the ladder to the hall where a fireman met me and put an oxygen mask over my face. The fire, the principal said later, started on the roof. The tar box had malfunctioned. That is how I remember the world catching fire.

I have worked with crews of men who fight fire with shovels and axes rather than fire. We dig and hack. We try to cover the advancing fingers in dirt and the fingers simply flick it off most of the time. We set firebreaks with flame throwers so the backdraft will stop a larger wall of flame from moving forward.

I think of my crew members when we have had to lie down in the bush and let the fire walk over us as we huddled beneath a silver blanket. Some of my friends have tried to hide from the flames and when we found them they had been touched by a night without a heaven above it because forests try to make their own stars when they shoot embers into the sky.

A charred tree is both horrible and fascinating. The outer layer of bark burns off and often exposes the watercourses beneath the skin. Those damp channels save the base of the tree so sometimes, a year or two after a forest fire has passed through, the strongest among them, mostly the old oaks and maples, sprout new shoots and try to restart their lives. The scar of the water channels that fire leaves behind resembles an open would in a torso. The intestines of the tree are bright orange and they twist in the pattern of a tangled hose that is both awe-inspiring and insidious to see. Everywhere and everything that has been touched by fire is both beautiful and horrific in a way that artists attempt to express the impossible vision of failure and success in one stunning work of art.

Fire does that whenever I find myself in the middle of it, surrounded and fighting for my life and digging non-stop to make a way out of the ring of fire. As I work and my entire body aches and sweat from exertion and the heat almost drowns me where I stand, I ask the flames why they want to change the landscape. The flames are the bristles in an artist's brush. They are painting a canvas that sums up the contradictions of this world – the analytical, calm, rational understanding of a flashlight and the chaotic rage of a stolen chariot.

When there is a parting in the smoke, and sometimes that is not a good sign because it means the wind is shifting and me and my crew might get caught in the wrong place, I look up at the sun as swoops low on bright yellow wings before dropping a load of lake water, fish and all, on the slope or the brush ahead of us. The flames speak their own language and they tell us what they want, and most of the time we cannot give it to them. They are greedy.

We are told to stand our ground, told to protect an important hydro clearing or a highway where people are frantic to get out of the way of the fire. I have traveled the world and as some people see beaches everywhere they go, I see flames. We become entrenched and refuse to budge. From there, we advance, even after dark, and continue our struggle in a new position the way soldiers struggle not merely to kill each other but to gain a tactical advantage. We aim to take the high ground.

When I see the glow from flames that are so bright and rising as starry embers in the night sky, I am certain the flickering can be seen on the other side of the world. The shadows that I am casting appear on the walls of frightened children who must be soothed to sleep and told the truth about what shadows are.

I often ask myself in the middle of a nightmare where the light is coming from if what I see is locked inside the darkness of my mind and my eyes are closed. I call that light the illusion of fire. It comes from nowhere and it shows us only what we are permitted to see the way a flashlight in the dark reveals only the morning side of a child's globe. That glow is what illumines their minds if they wake to the sound of hooves printing on the clouds of smoke and have no idea what they have heard or why the noise startled them from their sleep.

Guide

I have had a long time to think about what happened, how Tommy Gill turned and stuck his tongue out at me as he ran into the valley then vanished. It was my responsibility to walk him home from kindergarten

Tommy Gill started kindergarten late. His parents moved into the neighborhood during the mid-autumn of my Sixth grade. I was entrusted to be Tommy's guide. My responsibility was to walk him the eight blocks through the twists and turns of our suburb and deliver him to his front door.

Tommy knew very little about the suburb where we lived. The area was an intricate knot of streets. Some of the prestige lots backed onto a ravine, but the ravine didn't end where the houses stopped. The old river course went into a wilderness of overgrown bushes and scrub pine.

My older brother George said he would get lost in there even though he knew the paths he ran with the older boys. He told me there were hiding places in the bushes and 'forts' as he called them. He never showed them to me saying it was too dangerous. Criminals and bums loitered in the ravine. The older boys frequented the inaccessible places where they smoked or hung out and carve their initials on the trunks of trees or took girls down into the overgrowth where they would make out.

At first, Tommy accepted me and obeyed my instructions to keep up with me as I hurried home to catch the superhero cartoons. Sometimes he slowed me down.

He would hold up watercolor paintings he had done in art time each day, splashes of black and red paint. I was supposed to guess what they were, The first several days, I could tell what his brushwork attempted to depict and could name the object – house, school, tree, horse. But on the fifth day, I got the answer wrong. I had no idea what the splotch was supposed to be and because my response was incorrect Tommy told me I was stupid and I didn't know anything, not even the shorter way home.

I learned, years later, that another boy in Tommy's circle of friends showed off to him by insisting there was a shorter way home, a way that cut an extra half hour off the walk. I told my charge there was no shorter 'other' way home. We had to take a turn here or there and follow the road until it connected to another street. He wanted to go through the valley. That was the shortcut. I was stupid not to cut through the ravine. I told him my way was the safest but where the road bridged the creek with a tunnel overpass Tommy bolted down the hill.

The way down was icy. For Tommy, who was considerably lighter, the steep hill was a slide, and he went down it on his ass. I slipped on the way down as I chased him, calling his name, ordering him to come back, shouting he didn't know what lay ahead in the thickets and would get lost, freeze to death in the snow or, worse, meet up with one of the shadow men my brother had seen in the hollow.

Holding his artwork in one hand and a dangling red mitten on a string in the other, Tommy turned and stuck his tongue out at me, then ran into the thicket. I tried to follow him, but the sun sets early in mid-December and the shadows are long and purple and a five-year-old in a navy coat blends with the ghosts of trees and the dark outlines they cast on newly fallen snow. Within seconds, Tommy Gill was gone.

I thought I was running after him, but my footing went out from under me. I fell and hurt my back, When I reached the bottom where the creek argued with itself as it flowed between channels of ice and tried to force river stones out of its path, I stood and listened, hoping to hear the crunch of Tommy's steps in the boot-deep snow but all I heard was the creek and wind haunting the trees. Behind me, in the distance, a light from the kitchen of the last house threw a glow on the hillside.

I made my way up the incline. Hawthorn trees on the slope reached out and tore my coat as if someone had fought with me. One thorn put a gash in my cheek. That would be important.

I struggled because I kept slipping on the ice beneath the day's snowfall. I pounded on the side entrance of the house where the kitchen light shone. After banging on the aluminum storm door for what felt like an eternity but was only five minutes according to the woman who answered, the inner door opened a crack on the chain and a nose and a pair of eyes peered out at me, asking what I wanted, suspicious I was a hoodlum.

The woman began to close the door on me, to ignore me and pretend I wasn't there when, through tears, I cried and sputtered to describe how a little boy in my care might be in danger. All she heard of my plea was 'little boy.' She saw my jacket torn. She saw the blood on my face. She told me to stand where I was while she phoned the police. When she returned she asked what I had done to the child. I broke down and all I said was, 'He's gone.'"

My tears were my undoing.

The prosecuting attorney would point out my wild state of mind suggesting I knew the boy had come to harm, that I had lost control and done terrible things to him. How else could I have known something was wrong?

The police arrived with dogs and the search went long into the night.

I was taken home.

My father believed the police. He told me I was a 'no good kid.'

My mother told him he was wrong, insisting the school had chosen me over other boys to see the new arrival safely home.

The principal said he'd never had any trouble with me until then and had seemed a nice boy, and maybe he was wrong to have placed his trust in me.

A psychologist said I was disturbed. My father's rejection of me – even though my father was an alcoholic – had triggered 'problems, deep-seated anger, and a form of juvenile maladjustment that caused me to harm Tommy.'

The police said Tommy must have put up a fight. That's I got my gash. The prosecutor produced photos of Tommy's half-naked body, his artwork pinioned to a bare branch on a hawthorn, his neck turned in an awkward direction as if he were looking away from his attacker in disbelief. All I had to show in my defense was a fading bruise on my backside no one wanted to see.

My days in court were followed by years in detention where I was whipped by the warden for being hungry, beaten for being the last one out of my bed one morning, burned by an older boy's contraband cigarette for insisting I was innocent.

The boy said, 'no one is innocent in here. The court says so.'

The psychiatrist assigned to my case asked how I felt toward poor little Tommy. I said I wanted to smack him. Tommy Gill was a bad child, a little cuss who thought he knew better. I wanted my life back.

The sentence did not end when I reached my eighteenth birthday. Tommy's parents appeared at all my parole hearings and insisted I should rot in prison.

I am still in prison. I had my forty-sixth birthday yesterday.

When I was being transferred last week to a medium-security prison out west, we flew over the suburb where the streets wound around each other the way a tangled length of string or garden hose gets knotted into a puzzle no one can undo it. The streetlamps below had just been switched on. Their haloes fell on the snowy crescents and cul de sacs. The unlit ravine remained a wound cut across the neighborhood.

I can't say who killed Tommy Gill, but I confess I failed in my responsibility.

I should have grabbed him by the sleeve of his snowsuit and held him tight as if I were holding on to my own life. I accepted my responsibility and failed.

When I am awake at night I visualize Tommy Gill's last painting. Maybe it was a depiction of my future or his, a wash of black haphazardly brushed on the yellow manilla paper but I am just guessing.

I have heard of the valley of death from ministers who work with the inmates. They speak of real death, not the living death I know and wait to outlive.

Ten years ago George came to visit me. He said he knew the spot where Tommy had been found and visited it often. I asked George why he went back there. He shrugged and looked at his hands.

He wouldn't look me in the eye until he said what he came to say and even when he left he never glanced over his shoulder.

No one, according to my brother, bothered to remove Tommy's painting from the bough of the hemlock. It wasn't entered into evidence. It wasn't passed along to the boy's mother as a keepsake. It was still there, marking the spot I was supposed to have done the terrible thing. The rain and snow poured down on it and it wept black tears. If it is still there, it moves lifelessly as the wind pleases and by now must have found something different to depict. Maybe it is a picture of time.

Portrait

When the New Mercer Asylum was abandoned after the building had been condemned for age, the portrait of Dr. Benham was left behind. The painting, considered a reasonable likeness of the doctor, is troubling. The eyes move. There is a look of superiority on the sitter's face that says, "You are merely human and I am better than you."

Nailed high and mighty on the wall, the image seems to oversee even the slightest movement in the Refectory. The dining hall was the only room with ceilings high enough to accommodate the work's enormity and keep it beyond the reach of vandals. When it was unveiled those who knew the doctor said he had finally reached the lofty heights he accorded himself in his own mind. The truth was that even after Benham died and New Mercer was abandoned no one wanted the portrait.

Dr. Benham had no known relatives. His alma mater acquainted with his psychiatric practices refused it. The canvas depicted Dr. Benham in a white lab coat she never wore, preferring instead a green gardener's coverall, a seldom-used stethoscope in the breast pocket, and his infamous black book clutched in his right hand.

Benham considered himself a religious man, the hand of God, at least in his relationship with his patients. When someone under his treatment did not respond to the wet leather straight jacket that gradually dried and squeezed some sense into their heads, he would take the individual into the garden for a spiritual experience that included flagellation and crowns of thorns.

The asylum was a high point on tours of the region's abandoned buildings. The corridor walls and ceilings were shedding their plaster, and the relic that proved someone had entered the place was a tile from the pool room where the doctor insisted that difficult cases walk upon the waters even if they could not swim. Although his pronouncements and cures were kept strictly in-house, Dr. Benham had a theory that disorders were expressions of angelic possession. He was said to have cured an old man whose residency at New Mercer pre-dated his arrival in the late Forties. The man was drawing sigils in the dust on a window sill, and Mercer made similar unusual marks with his fingertip and the man smiled, and said, "You're one of us." Benham released the old man that day, fired the cleaning staff, and was present in a rotten orchard when the police cut down the former patient's body.

People who visited New Mercer tried their best to deface the portrait. They threw handfuls of fallen plaster at the uncanny stare when the eyes followed them around the empty hall. Nothing seemed to damage the painting. The Refectory doubled as an activity area. There was a rumor that one young man who Benham had deemed incorrigible was nailed to a cross there after breaking a loaf of bread into small pieces and feeding each patient. The young man told them they would be healed, and miraculously produced a bottle of wine and made each of the inmates drink from it. No one knew how the spirits had passed through security and when questioned the young man replied simply, "This is my blood given to you."

The beginning of the end came when the families of those who resisted Benham's treatments began to question what had become of their kin. Benham stood before a regulatory board and insisted though his mansion, as he called New Mercer, had many rooms, it only had room enough for one king. Realizing the asylum was dilapidated and beyond repair and still bore all the hallmarks of the bedlams to which people had been consigned in the Nineteenth century, the decision was made to shutter New Mercer. There wasn't money enough to tear it down.

As for Dr. Benham, there was one rumor that circulated in town where he was an odd shadow who appeared and disappeared as if he was without substance, dwelling among the people but refusing to respond to their expressions of cordialities. Word spread that he was the doctor of souls who despised people, and despising them in their flesh, tortured the spirits that harbored within them. No matter how many angelic faces pass through the doors of psychiatric institutions, confused and confounded by the miseries of this world that run contrary to their way of dealing with reality, there will always be a Dr. Benham. Prophets drive the world to the verge of destruction but false prophets make sure catastrophe is fulfilled.

Then, one day, he was gone. The police, lacking enthusiasm for Benham's disappearance and investigating his whereabouts by only going through the motions found the doctor in the asylum garden. He was clutching a bag of silver half dollars as he dangled from the bough of an oak tree that had been struck repeatedly by lightning. From the appearance of what remained of the body, the tree must have been blasted while Benham dangled from it.

Even in death his eyes bulged and appeared to move as those below him moved, just as they did in the painting, glaring at people with a look of superiority on his face. His black book in which he recorded the sins of his patients for future reference and surprise punishment had been stuffed in his mouth. He could have been mistaken in his long green gardener's smock for a skein of moss though such things do not grow around New Mercer, and the sign into the town has been vandalized in anger or a warning to others. It reads *Non-Miser*, a joke scrawled by someone familiar with Latin, which in the context of the New Mercer Asylum translates as 'there is misery here.'

Rare Flower (Fiction North)

Abebe wanted to be a poet. Poetry speaks of flowers, she told her mother who smiled and went back to preparing the wat. She wanted to give her voice to the meadows. The meadows were alive with flowers after the months of rain. The world was alive but it couldn't tell anyone because no one had given it words to speak.

When she was a small child, there was an old man who would sit in the shade of a large tree near the well and sing poems. There was nothing she would rather do than sit and listen to his voice. Her mother told her she was being useless and wasting her time, but the inflections rising and falling made her feel as if she was riding on the clouds.

One day he asked her what her name was.

"Abebe," she answered. "It means rare flower."

"I know that," said the old man. He began a song about a mountain flower that was more beautiful than any in the world. A young man sought it out, not to pluck it, but to lie down beside it and inhale its perfume. But to reach the flower on the mountain, the young man had to endure many trials and tests.

Before the poem could end, the old man vanished.

Long after the village had been torn apart by warring factions, and after her mother wandered off into the sand to find help for her young brother and never returned, and after the flies had closed his eyes, Abebe made her way to a camp where an Irishman bandaged her feet. He sent her to a place that was so cold the constant rain ate into her bones.

Her teachers did not take her poetry seriously, especially when she wrote about a doll she owned. Her mother made it for her. The rag baby was dressed in flowers, and though it always appeared dead when someone else held it, Abebe knew it sang to her in whispers.

"Do you still have it?" the teacher asked.

"No," she said as she wept. "Only its words."

Princess and Rick

Rick was everything she wanted in a man. He was tall, caring, and compassionate. The look in his eyes and the depth in his voice said, "I'm the only one who can care for you." He stroked her hair and called her Princess, and yet her parents were surprised when she announced she was moving out and going to live with Rick.

She'd found a cozy apartment for herself and her beloved on the other side of the city – close enough to stay in contact with her parents but just that extra mile for her to live her dream life with Rick undisturbed. The first night together in their new place she decided to surprise him with her cooking skills. Lasagna was a specialty of hers. She bought into the adage that the way to a man's heart was through his stomach though she wondered if that were anatomically possible.

But he didn't want anything. He wasn't hungry. The food sat on the plate and grew cold. Maybe some ingredient in the entrée put him off. He got up and left. The door slammed. She cried herself to sleep alone in their bed.

Her mother phoned the next morning. They were close and always spent Saturday mornings together at the farmer's market. Immediately, her mother detected there was something wrong with her daughter – a lump in the voice, a raspiness that suggested the young woman had been weeping. Mothers read emotional pain. But Rick's Princess insisted everything was fine.

On Sunday morning she was surprised by a knock at the door. Her mother was holding a bouquet and her father carried a basket of apples. She couldn't turn them away even if they had arrived unannounced. She wanted the company even if she could not admit it.

Her father excused himself and asked to use the washroom while mother and daughter sat on the couch, talking as if there was nothing wrong and life with Rick was going through a period of adjustment and would, eventually, be everything she dreamed if not more.

Alone in the washroom, he noticed that only his daughter's dressing gown hung on the hook behind the door. He opened the medicine cabinet. He didn't want to pry but he was curious what kind of man Rick was. Was Rick a cheap aftershave guy who would splash an electric scent of blue liquid on his face and race to work or was his daughter's ideal partner someone who indulged in expensive sandalwood cologne, a sure sign of extravagance and self-importance. He didn't want his daughter to break her heart.

But when he opened the medicine cabinet and scanned the shallow shelves for a razor or any sign of male presence there was nothing but two bottles – Aspirin and

Midol. A lone pink toothbrush rested in a tumbler. His heart sank because he knew all perfect men eventually leave, and if they were perfect they may never have existed at all.

How to Draw a Frog
(Editor's Prize, Edinburgh Flash Fiction Prize)

Successful artists ensure the frog is not dead. A live frog adds a degree of verity to the drawing process. The artist must be quick to capture the impulsive movements of the subject. Frogs are easily distracted. Inert, docile amphibians are best but hard to find.

Avoid dead frogs. They lack something, not just their lives. That goes without saying. They lose that glint in their eyes. They're easier to work with but are specimens rather than subjects. The virescent depth of their green fades. If a frog is too dead the drawing is no longer of a frog but something returning to the mulch at the bottom of the pond. Such frogs aren't satisfactory subjects.

Some artists find success by capturing frogs in their habitat but if the creatures – frog and artists – are handled too aggressively terror ensues. Everything has a level of delicacy both artist and subject must respect. The best frogs appear happy with their circumstances. Happiness is difficult to detect but the longer a frog is studied the more its happiness becomes apparent.

Keeping a frog happy is hard work. A good artist must put a smile on the face of a little, green, Mona Lisa. Keeping company with other frogs is not enough. The best practice is to raise a frog from a tadpole to a complete frog so frog and artist can trust each other in a lasting bond where a happy artist draws, and a skilled frog poses.

Every Day

Every day, it's a getting' closer
Goin' faster than a roller coaster
Love like ours will surely find a way,
Heh-hay, he-hay…

Buddy Holly

Light in the universe is rare. Light requires the presence of a myriad of atomic explosions within a star or the reflection of those cataclysms on the surface of lightless bodies. In between those engines of action and reaction exists an expanse where nothing happens, where voices are not heard, and where the shape of matter is in a constant state of flux.

I came home and sat down on my bed when I learned about light and dark in science class. I wept. I asked myself why daylight was so brief, why time was measured in the constant sunrises of our lives, and where hope could find a place to exist without the darkness chasing it away. That moment was a profound revelation to me. Every day I try to hold on to a little bit more of what enables me to see the world I live in and if that weren't enough of a challenge everything around me changes with every second.

My mother wanted me to get help. I was only nine years old. Older members of the family who did not understand told me I thought too much. My Uncle Gary, the consoler-general of our clan, said I shouldn't worry about it, that I needed to live life as it came to me and there was nothing I could do to alter the way the universe works.

When I was twelve I woke one winter morning with the idea that perhaps that reality was an illusion, the I obeyed rules I didn't make, and that there is always light in the world, somewhere, always a sunrise, and always a night but with a little bit of effort on my part I could alter the course of things. I could make light the predominant expression of the cosmos.

I didn't want to tell anyone – at least not until I figured out how I could change the rules and make daylight the perpetual gift we all could receive. Our church minister had told me only God could change the way time and physics work. The disparity between light and darkness, after all, had been by His design, and that boys my age should rise early, use the precious daylight to read and study so we wouldn't strain our eyes, and then go to bed early because that would make me healthy, wealthy, and wise. My mother had that saying on a Torquay ware candlestick. The motto had never meant anything to me until the Reverend said I ought to obey God's work.

Then I asked who God was. He didn't like the question. "Could God be any of us?" I said.

He told me I was speaking blasphemy. He said we all wear God's image, meaning we look like him because the human race was His family, and he cited a philosopher named Emmanuel Levinas who argued that each of us bears the mark of divinity because we are made in God's image.

I asked the Reverend that if that was so if we looked like "Our Heavenly Father," would we not also inherit some of his skills? I look like my father. My mother says so. My father is very good with tools. He spends long hours at his workbench in the basement fixing broken mechanical objects. He saved my alarm clock when it fell on the floor. Like that? I asked the Reverend. The man of God just shook his head and walked away.

Maybe he didn't want to reveal trade secrets. That had to be it. Each of us inherited not only our looks from God's side of the family but also the inclinations (a word I looked up in a dictionary) or predispositions (a word I found under the same definition) to be able to do certain things. So, if God was light, another of the catchphrases I heard in church, and God made the light, then maybe I had the power to make it too or at least to encourage its co-operation with the way I wanted things to be.

I started practicing. At first, I realized that calling the sun to rise a few minutes earlier each day was kind of stupid because, after the Winter Solstice, the days get longer so the planet can warm up and enjoy some nice summer days. The careful notes and tables I created during the winter were suddenly wrong, at least scientifically, and the real test of my will would come after the Summer Solstice in June, which in reality doesn't mark the beginning of summer at all because everything is in bloom by then. My mother is already picking her cherry tomatoes and cutting them up into salads.

On the morning of June 22, I rose early (with the help of the alarm clock my father was able to salvage) and I stared at the northeastern horizon where I knew the sun would come up. The day should have started later but instead, the sun came up early by about five minutes. The sudden change in the time of sunrise made the news but I wasn't ready to make any claims for my skills.

All summer long, I repeated the experiment and got amazing results – not the same results which would have been a form of insanity but sunrises that came earlier and earlier. Then I set to work on the sunsets and got an even better reply from the universe. The days were longer and longer. The problem was that too much sunlight made the summer a scorcher but I wasn't going to stop training myself.

There were complaints to the local and national media that starlight was becoming more difficult to see, that something had gone wrong with the universe. My answer, had anyone asked me, would have been that nothing was wrong. I was just correcting a situation where darkness was the prevailing presence in the heavens.

Then, one day, after I had stayed up not just all night but for three days and my mother was worried I was hallucinating and thought I had gone manic, I did it. I flipped the structure of the night. The stars, except for our Sun, became pinpoints of darkness in the night and the darkness became bright. The crew from the Space Station discovered they could take off their helmets and talk to each other where, before I learned to use my skills inherited from God, they would have drifted in an empty and lightless void and their heads would have exploded into the vacuum of space.

But I hadn't anticipated the effect perpetual light would have on the universe. Grasslands and forests burst in flames. The sea began to boil. The Reverend said it was the "End of Days." And I realized, perhaps too late to save many people, that the starry night sky served a purpose – that the light of stars, so distant and lonely – made days, however few they were worth living and worth seeing. The sunrise, I decided, was a flashbulb like the kind Uncle Gary used on his vintage camera when he took family pictures.

We would line up, as he asked, and arrange ourselves with the creases smoothed out of the aunts' dresses and the men's shirt collars straight, and we would smile. We would smile and say "Cheese," and show our teeth because in that brief pop of life we were saying everything we possibly could say about life. We were saying, "Here we are in this moment, a moment on a summer afternoon that we will not live again and look at how happy we are even if we weren't, and how we long to exist forever if we could only hold the light in hands the way I cupped fireflies in the dark and their tiny behinds glowed because they wanted other fireflies to know they were there."

I had to go to a lot of work to put the night back in the sky. I wanted to write an apology letter to the people on the other side of the world but even if I wrote it they probably wouldn't bother to read it or want to read it. The document, a world-changing statement, would just be to them some piece of garbage penned by a kid who was probably out of his mind.

What I learned – and this sounds like the sort of essay teachers expect everyone to write on the first day back to school after a long summer – "What I Did on My Summer Vacation" – was why the stars appear tiny in the night, and so small and so few compared to what surrounds them. Maybe God really is love and light, and if love is hard to find so is light. A person has to look for it. Too much love and light aren't good and the fact there isn't much of either to go around complicates things. The stars are infinite but so is the darkness and in terms of proportion there is more absence of light than presence. That's sad but that's just the way things are and for a good reason.

I have to look hard for love and light though there are times when I am with my family I can't help but feel the whole house or cottage is full of their shining expressions.

The following summer I decided to pursue a new skill. I began my study of waves and whether water was liquid or merely an illusory absence of solidity. After all, glass is a liquid and I have seen pictures in magazines of rooms and swimming pools where people installed glass floors – surfaces they can walk on. The question of density is the fly in the ointment but I am working on a way around that. Water became my new passion as the world returned to normal and my family, Uncle Gary included, spread themselves on towels in the sun on a long, sandy beach where the ocean sparkled with millions of tiny stars twinkling and thanking me for giving them their brief months of freedom and the opportunity to know why they must remain so rare.

Afternoon
(Heartwood Literary Magazine)

You posed with your arms slung over each other's shoulders, holding fish in your free hands with a dock in the background.

I never knew my own father. But yours? He was a father you were close to, a father who would listen, who'd be there, an 'old man' who would tell you what's what but in a kind way. A father who took you out for a damned fine steak on your eighteenth birthday because you were a man and steak is what men eat. A man who stood you a drink as if you were an old friend.

Sister Macklin said he'd hang on for the rest of the afternoon and a can of warm pop and a questionable sandwich of dried-out white bread and a slice of ham was all the respite you were given. The generators had failed. The corridors were sweltering. Ices melted in the freezer. The tea and coffee machines weren't working, and though it was a hot day everything you touched was cold. I tried to take your hand but you turned to me and said, "No."

We'd only just pulled the tabs on the warm Cokes. We'd only just taken one horrifying bite from the sandwich when Sister Macklin appeared, her black hair rolled under her white nurse's cap, her forehead sweating from doing the flights of stairs and the return trip awaiting us as we had to navigate the stairwells lit by dim evacuation lights to the seventh floor, all so we could look upon a man who was no longer there. The dying leave us breathless.

You entered the room. The sister, perhaps to spare you or give you a moment that is so important between a father and son – not between a father and son and the son's boyfriend – was right out of *Hamlet*.

You had to go in alone. You had to cradle the truth in your arms, tilting the head this way and that, saying nothing but pain nonetheless.

You had to be told the truth of his demise straight from his spirit. I felt as if you'd walked into the fog on a battlement and a horrible truth was about to be revealed to you. That's all it was. The truth. It wasn't horrible. It just was the truth.

I never told you that just before you left his room and stood talking in a low voice to the sister, I went to him and opened one of his eyes and I was the last thing he saw or didn't see. He probably didn't see me. If he had, I would have felt I violated your relationship with him.

The eye did not look at me as much as through me. I asked his forgiveness but none was forthcoming. How could it? He'd said all he had to say during his life. It wasn't forgiveness. It was just acceptance. The way he accepted his own death. The way he believed he would never see a grandchild of his own. It was just a loneliness. Isolation. Living with so many ends unanswered for, so many threads that could not be neatly tied up into a neat conclusion he dreamed of knowing in his isolation. It was abandonment. You were there, but no matter how close you stood, leaning over him the night before so he could whisper secrets in your ear, he was abandoned. And he abandoned you because that's the way death leaves things.

His face had collapsed in on itself, his false teeth taken out for mercy's sake, and the round O of his mouth caked with what looked like dried oatmeal but is the crap that comes out of the mouths of the dying.

I looked in that one eye. It wasn't seeing anything. It was just there, staring. But as we climbed up the fourteen staircases, sixteen if you count the fact the cafeteria is in the basement, I heard you growing short of breath, huffing, and then the sound of a sob, your shoulders going up, and your hand gripping the stair rail. I thought, "Don't hold back on my account. Don't show me your grief if you aren't." I was the jealous lover that Keith Douglas describes in his poem about the dead Panzer man in the burned-out tank. *Vergissmeinnicht.* I don't remember the lines and even if I did you would hate me for thinking of them.

I wished we'd all gone fishing together. I wanted more than anything to have been a better part of your life. I could see what I had missed, what I could never understand. Long conversations. Steak on my eighteenth birthday. The advice poured shot by shot at the kitchen table.

And as you stood there weeping into your hand, standing like a shadow over the body of your father, I could picture you and me together, maybe not in the past but someday, somewhere, maybe if we had a kid of our own, and we'd be standing there with our arms around each other's shoulder, the little guy proudly holding up the undersized fish we caught and should have thrown back, and some guy hanging around the dock we hand our camera to and hearing him say, "Smile" and clicking the shutter because it all is over in the blink of an eye. And what we fail to love or be loved by makes us see what we have or should have had, or ought to hold on to even though it is slippery and it fought for its life on the end of a thin line. And as an afterthought, after the hook is removed from the fish's mouth, you persuade the child that all things deserve the lives they have struggled to live. You lie flat on your stomach and lower your hands over the side of the dock. The fish is inanimate. It stares at the sky. And then, to the boy's amazement and yours, its opens and closes a gill as it is submerged, its tail awakens, and it disappears into depths we will never completely understand.

The Toll

I wanted to be a shadow when I grew up. The light from the bathroom of our apartment shone in the door of my room, and when my mother thought I was asleep, I would make shadow puppets on the wall. The rooster from my grandparent's farm always had a conversation with the spider who lived in the toolshed where my grandfather would sharpen his ax on a grindstone and repair harnesses for horses he hadn't seen in sixty years.

My grandfather's life, at least as much as I knew of the only father figure I had during my childhood, was rural and simple. There were dangers in what he did but the dangers were caused by moments of carelessness – a fall from a hayloft, a misplaced stroke of a cross-cut saw. The old man would take my hand as we walked through fields to his woodlot astride a creek. He shaped his hands and gave voices to his shadows animals.

My grandfather said, "If you want to become a shadow, you have to know how to make them."

We invented stories of dogs, cats, spiders, mice, and a rooster with a comb atop its head. I asked the shadow where it was from and why it was such a long way from the sea, and the shadow replied it lived in the harbor and someday I would raise my open eyes to the sky and follow it as it circled upwards toward the sun.

A barn cat pawed at a mouse. A rooster crowed in a bright morning. Then I saw a hand reach into the light and form a seagull.

The hand was neither mine nor my grandfather's, and it wasn't attached to an arm. When my grandfather left my room,

I wondered where this extra hand had come from. My fingers could not shape that way.

People said I had my father's eyes. They claimed I was the image of him, the shadow of the boy he once was. I told them I was not a shadow but always added that I had my grandfather's hands. My grandfather's broad palms and strong fingers were shadows of a life spent toiling with nature, repelling the forces of circumstance, so at the end of each day, he felt a small victory had been won in his fields or his tractor shed.

When a pastor asked, "O death where is thy victory?" I never counted my grandfather among the victims. The father I mourn but never knew was felled by circumstances he could not control.

The bell tolls until all the names have been read, and because our last name begins with W, I have to wait and keep my eyes closed for what feels like forever. When I open them and raise my gaze to where the towers once stood, I see the gull as it circles in an updraft. And for a moment the bird becomes the hand that wasn't mine floating above my shadow animals.

Day of the Dead

Annie was aching to see Pedro. She needed him so very much. His absence felt like death and her empty arms were almost numb from the pain of missing him.

Pedro lived in Galeana on the other side of the grey saw-teeth of the Sierra Madres In the late afternoon light with the sun behind them, they traced the jagged outline of an enormous beast with a rough back. The nearer she approached, the greener slopes became. She had been warned not to drive alone over the Sierras on her own.

"A woman alone in a car," the man at the rental agency had said in a whisper as he leaned over the counter.

The road snaked through the mountains. The shoulders were narrow and in some places non-existent, especially on the turns, and if she had to pull over for any reason – goats crossing the road, a flat tire, or simply to admire the green view on the steep valleys on the lush Caribbean side or the bone-colored hills facing the interior once she went over the crest – she would be watched at every moment by cartel snipers.

"Why make a target of yourself?" the rental man asked.

Pedro had argued with her over the phone, the line cutting in and out. "Stay at an airport hotel. Don't make the journey alone. It is four hours from Monterrey. Why pay for a rental car? I can come and get you in the morning."

The thought of Pedro arriving in Galeana with an Englishwoman frightened her. The narrow streets, the shops where nothing much was sold because nothing much was purchased, the relatives crowded into a cinder-block room, the whirr and clunk of the malfunctioning air conditioner, were things she did not want to encounter. Pedro had made it out of that world. He was a telecom engineer. He traveled the world and earned good money. They'd met in Zurich. Pedro, dark, suave, the epitome of Latin elegance and refined manners, and she, the clever Oxbridge technologist who knew all the answers except the ones she was working to find. They fell in love while having drinks and conversation about 5G. They both agreed they held the future in their hands.

But the more he attempted to convince her, the more assertive she felt she had to be. After all, he was not only in love with her. Love is a reciprocal arrangement. If she let him have his way on how she came to him, he would have his way on everything.

She'd been to Galeana once already on a brief trip. It seemed a dream to her. There was a village she wanted to see again. She had fallen in love with it as they walked hand-in-hand through the ancient streets.

Iturbide stood on the crest of the highway. It was shady and green, the last breath of the verdant before the descent began and the Joshua Palms with sea urchin spines stood amazed and abandoned to die in the desert.

And it was the day of the dead.

What better place to see the shrines and the Calaveras in the quiet square than Iturbide. People with faces painted as skulls, white, morbid, and surprised by death, would be kneeling in the square, offering shot glasses of reposado to their ancestors and reminding themselves of those whose features had faded from memory by placing sugar skulls on the cenotaphs. So many never returned to the mountain village.

She was almost certain she was entering Iturbide. As she slowed her rental and rolled down the windows, she could hear the bell tolling for vespers. An old woman in a blue skirt would be tugging at the lone bell-rope that hung as if it were the snake from paradise creeping down the white stucco tower of the church. The front wall over the door would be red with bougainvillea and she imagined the Crown of Thorns, the suffering and blood that defined the Mexico she loved as the fluttering red petals. If the wind came up, they would scatter, pulsing from a sacrificial wound.

But she was not in Iturbide. Not the Iturbide she remembered. There has been a town hall at the far end of the square. A youth dance had taken place after school. Pedro explained it was a way to keep the young people in the sleepy town. They would grow up, marry. They would live in one of the old, low, brightly colored houses on the side street. She'd seen couples and their children, making their way up a side street and she understood how important love is when it is asked to bind people not only to one another but to a place.

Pedro and she sat on a park bench and talked about death.

"There is no death for us, at least not the way you see it, Annie. You've been taught to grieve for what is lost permanently. We have been taught to respect and worship those who are dead. Each year, the day after your Halloween, we have the Day of the Dead. We call upon the saints, but we also call upon those who walk with the saints in the twilight of a dusty autumn day. My grandmother, my father, my aunts, and uncles, all live in that twilight. When you return, I hope you will return on the Day of the Dead, and I will introduce you to them all and you will hear them speak to you in the silence."

When she parked the car she was certain she was not in Iturbide. Had she taken a wrong turn? Highway 58 leads directly to Iturbide. There could be no mistaking it. All she had to do was follow the road toward the sky and then leave the sky behind. The church was not where she remembered it. The square had fewer trees. The bell-rope ran inside the church rather than dangle free on the outside. She missed the bright red flowers.

A group of women with their backs turned to her, black shawls over their heads, and long dresses with elaborate embroidery were kneeling beside a shrine, laying kernels of colored corn on the ground in the pattern of a multicolored flower. As Annie approached, she thought it odd that the women were picking the sugar Calaveras from the shrine and eating them. From what she knew of the tradition, the candy sugar skulls were only for the dead. Another woman reached up and took a shot glass of tequila that stood beside a faded antique photograph of a man and downed the drink in one mouthful.

"Perdóneme. ¿Es esto Iturbide?"

One of the women, her face deathly pale as the bleached sands of the desert, her eyes blacked out, and her teeth painted on her lips and cheeks as if death had stripped away her flesh looked up at Anne and said nothing.

The bell was tolling. The women who kneeled at the shrine picked up their skirts and ran toward a process as it left the church. Annie followed. The procession moved slowly.

The priest at the head of the line was swinging his sensor. The smoke was sweet, almost sickly, but it held a bitter tang as if it were smoke that had been retrieved from the ceiling of a church after a mass and mixed with the scent of cigars and cooking and chocolate that had boiled over into the fire.

No one spoke. Everyone's head was bowed. The silence, the reverence of a dusk when not a bird chirped or a rustle of a long dress could be heard, was mesmerizing. Annie wanted to embrace it. She felt as if it was a part of her that lay waiting in her soul that she had not yet discovered. And when the gate on the cemetery opened with a cry, Annie could see the arid plain below her, the graves packed as tightly as white bags of sugar, and each resting place was decorated in a photograph of the deceased and flowers, and seeds, the sugar Calaveras.

The priest, who was also in a calavera face, raised his arms, and the women, the men, the children moved toward the graves until they were standing on top of them. An elderly man and a woman embraced. A man put his arm around the boy and the boy, with blackened eyes, looked up at the man. A woman held a sleeping child in her arms. All had the white faces of the day painted over their flesh. And with that, they sank into the resting places and vanished as the sun sank over the village and the sky became dark.

Annie sank to her knees and began to pray for the dead. She wanted to whisper words of thanks but was overwhelmed and astonished by the silence. And when she opened her eyes, she was alone among the graves. The white paint had worn off the stones and the crosses. The monuments were toppled, and the walls were rubble. There was no priest, no flowers, no brightly colored petals, no sugar skulls or shot glasses of tequila or small loaves of bread for the dead. Even the vista of the arid plain to Galeana was shrouded in fog.

As she made her way back to her car, the village, the church, the side streets were in ruins. The square was empty. The shrine was gone. This was not Iturbide. Whatever this place was or had been left her feeling cold and empty inside. Had she taken a wrong turn?

She had no idea where she was.

Doubling back the way she came, as the darkness deepened, she kept checking her cell phone to see if she had any signal. She would call Pedro. She would describe the place where she had stopped. He could direct her or come for her.

She thought she heard his voice on the phone as she pulled off at a white roadside shrine in the valley. The shrine lay at the foot of an Aztec or Toltec rockface carving of a hunter. Pedro had told her it was an ancient prince who claimed the green valley as his private hunting preserve. The figure, known as Antares, had slid from the mountainside one day when an earthquake shook the valley. Nothing remained except the carving of a foot and a dog barking at the hooves of a deer.

"Pedro? Hello? Can you hear me?" He was breaking up. Only parts of words reached her. "I'm lost. I took a wrong turn. I lost something in myself and for a moment I was certain I found it. I found it in this village that vanished around me. Hello?"

The only words that came through were "San Sebastian" and "bridge."

She sat in the rental car and wept. San Sebastian? She scanned the map the man at the rental agency had given her as he warned her about traveling alone on Highway 58 from Linares to Galeana.

"That is a difficult route. You would be advised to go all the way back to Monterrey and cross the Sierras there. The way south, even though it is less picturesque and through the desert, is the safest. The truckers use that route unless they are in a hurry."

There was no San Sebastian on the map.

When she was a teenager, Annie stayed up all night with an elderly aunt in the Midwest US who was addicted to Broadway musicals. A late show called Midnight Matinee on a channel almost out of reach of her aunt's television antenna was playing the almost forgotten Rogers and Hammerstein musical, Brigadoon, about a Scottish village that only appears once every two hundred years because it is cursed. The only thing that can break the curse is if someone, on the right day, stumbles across the town and falls in love with a certain woman. The townsfolk are destined to fade in and out of eternity. Annie tried to imagine what eternity would feel like – the cold, the endless darkness, the wind on an autumn night pulling the temperature down from the sun and casting it into the grave. The feeling of nothing except longing. The love that was always on the other side of the mountain and, as in a dream, the road that would not lead to that love no matter how many times a person traveled it.

San Sebastian. Annie pictured a martyr, tied to a tree, being shot with arrows. His suffering eyes. She had seen paintings of him in the National Gallery. The young man with curly hair has his eyes raised to heaven as if asking when his suffering will end, when will he walk among the dead, and what the bridge is between this world and the next.

Annie thought for a moment that Mexico contained the secret of what that bridge was. Moving from death to life and back again, crossing the vast void with every sense – sight, sound, taste, touch, and smell with the volume turned up as high as it could go and blaring the world into every thought – was not just a matter of standing on one's own grave and eating the sweet marzipan skulls that were only fit for the dead, but a desire to assert love even if it meant negating the self in white face paint, and flowers woven in black braids of hair and permitting death to enter the world so it can live forever. She closed her eyes and thought she was dreaming when she opened them, to the sight of children in bright paper costumes, their faces painted white, their teeth outlined in black upon their cheeks, and their eyes two sockets of darkness with eclipses in the center of each. Each of them held out their hands as if asking for alms or inviting her to dance with them.

Eleanor

Her father never hung Mexican fly strips because he believed the insects were tiny demons and chased them around the house with a fly swatter. The walls, especially in the summer when the barnyard was ripe, were splattered with splotches of legs and wings. When her mother tried to rub them off with a rag and Dutch Cleanser, her father shook the woman violently by the wrist and insisted that leaving the bodies, like writing on the wall from the Old Testament, would serve as a warning to other flies, though the admonitions never worked and the house filled up with the insects day after day until Eleanor found it impossible to sleep even when she pulled a pillow over her head.

Now that she was out on her own with "No hope of ever going back," her father's words, she hung up a Mexican fly strip beside the desk in the room Bob found for her on Curtis Street with Mrs. Carlisle so the insects wouldn't buzz annoyingly when Eleanor went on Facebook. Bob was her rescuer. The people at the truck stop agreed there was something wrong with the way her father hit her and hit her hard as Eleanor screamed she was being abducted. Mrs. Carlisle was her guardian. They told Eleanor she was safe but could no longer be Eleanor Bane.

Mrs. Carlisle recorded her conversations with Eleanor's permission. Eleanor wanted to make sure that even if something happened to her others would know what she had been through. Mrs. Carlisle assured Eleanor that nothing would happen to her, that she and Bob and the organization would do everything they could to protect her. The organization gave girls like Eleanor their freedom.

It gave them their lives, taught them to read and write, and how to become part of the world they had been denied. The struggle for such young women was not merely leaving the homes and families they had known but leaving behind the identities they had been given. Many of the girls were only eighteen or nineteen. Bob wondered how Eleanor had lasted to twenty-three.

"No one wanted to marry me," she said. "They told me I was worthless and would make a poor wife. I had to watch as the girls I knew when I was younger became the sixth or seventh wives of men who were old enough to be my grandfathers. I told everyone I did not want children. They inspected me. There may have been some reason why I could not bear children. The old men said I was barren."

Bob told her that out here, in the real world, that didn't matter. Children were her choice. Eleanor had trouble understanding that, but she trusted Bob. Bob was her friend but he wasn't on Facebook. Mrs. Carlisle wasn't on Facebook either. Bob said his line of work didn't permit him to have social media pages and that Mrs. Carlisle flew beneath the radar, whatever that was, so girls like Eleanor would stand a chance once they broke free and got out into the world.

Eleanor wasn't sure what social media was. It sounded like a party. When she asked Bob if Facebook was a party he smiled and said it had been built for that but now it was often a dangerous neighborhood where people attacked one another, and Eleanor didn't want to be attacked anymore. She wasn't permitted to post pictures of herself which was fine because she didn't have any. Her hair had been dyed brown and cut short so they told her she looked like a pixie, and she wasn't sure what a pixie was either. Her name was Mindy now. Mindy Smith.

That's what it said on her name tag from happy land where she put her dyed hair in a brown net fitted over with a wrap-around brim to shade her eyes instead of a full brown baseball cap. If Mindy thought she recognized someone from her past, Bob showed her the way to drop her chin, hunch her shoulders, and look away. The boys on the job who joked with her got to wear full baseball caps. Mindy Smith's job was to keep the floors swept and mopped and to unload cartons of burgers and plastic bags of fries as the line cooks ran out. Eleanor didn't mind. Being someone else most of the week was a relief. She was busy and useful and Mr. Gallard who own the restaurant told her she was diligent. That meant focused. He showed his gratitude by handing Mindy a cheque that Mrs. Carlisle would deposit into an account for Eleanor so that when all the fuss blew over there'd be a nest egg, like a robin's, waiting for her so she could start a life where she didn't have to look over her shoulder. At the end of each day, Eleanor returned to her room when Mrs. Carlisle came to pick her up.

"We have to practice discretion," Mrs. Carlisle said. "Even though you are over the age of majority," whatever that meant, "we still brought you across state lines and because we're out of state they may come for you. The laws are different here than where you were," Mrs. Carlisle said. "The Children are looking for you and they won't give up until they find you and drag you back whether you want to be dragged back or not."

Facebook was full of faces but it was a lonely place. The Children didn't permit her to have Facebook but she had heard some of the girls in the compound giggling about it behind their hands so when Eleanor arrived at Mrs. Carlisle's house she asked if she could have Facebook and Mrs. Carlisle said, "Sure," because there was an old laptop kicking around that ought to do the trick and she sat down and taught Eleanor how to go online.

Eleanor giggled because the only thing she'd ever seen online was a fish her brother Roger caught in the creek back home before their father renamed him Isaac and wouldn't permit him to wear a hat when they worked in the fields. She didn't have any friends on Facebook except for the boy in Nigeria who wanted to marry her. She wasn't sure he was sincere and she told him she didn't have the money to fly him over so they could proceed with the necessary steps before matrimony. Maybe someday but not right now. Then he stopped being her friend. Making friends was difficult.

Learning to read was even harder. Mrs. Carlisle took pity on her one day and taught Eleanor how to sign her name so she could make bona fide applications for work. Eleanor didn't know what bona fide meant. It sounded slightly evil but she sensed Mrs. Carlisle meant well. The letters looped around each other like tangled vines in the weeds beside the stream back home.

When the flies came into Eleanor's room, Mrs. Carlisle gave her a Mexican fly strip and Eleanor thanked her and said she learned a lot about them by watching them die slowly. Mrs. Carlisle was surprised but not surprised. Eleanor explained that when she lived on a farm everything was about life and death and the things that die seldom stand a chance against the things that live. The Lord Almighty did not distinguish who or what should survive because everything was in His hands and most of the time His fist was clenched because He was a task-master Almighty who made people do His bidding or he'd smite them and they would bide no more. Eleanor told Mrs. Carlisle the story of her father and how he had driven his family beyond the reach of God in his pursuit of holiness only to bring them back, closer, and closer, to the nearness of the Lord because He must be obeyed as one obeys an earthly father no matter what.

The summer Eleanor was ten her earthly father came in from the cornfield late one hellfire of an afternoon. He hadn't worn his hat and had been working in the sun since dawn. His bald head was sunburnt and blazing red, although Eleanor wasn't sure she could say something was blazing on account of blazing being associated with you- know-where down there as she pointed to the floor. Her father told the family he had a vision. The Lord had called to him.

Eleanor wasn't sure there had been a voice.

The hogs had been restless and noisy all morning because an oil company was fracking nearby and the ground shook and shifted and part of the cornfield toppled sideways and fell into a hollow in the ground just before the pump water turned a filthy color that was probably the work of you-know-who as she pointed to the floor again.

Her father held up a glass of the water that had been clear and tasty the day before and pointing to it hollered at Eleanor and her mother that they had poisoned the Lord's blessing with their blood. Eleanor wasn't sure what he meant.

"We must leave this place of sin. We must seek out our kind so that we may be cleansed."

Mrs. Carlisle said, "Go on. This is interesting," and set a glass of lemonade in front of Eleanor as they sat at the kitchen table.

Eleanor thanked her and said her father used to hit her if she went on, but Mrs. Carlisle insisted she wouldn't hit her.

When her father came in from the corn, Eleanor's mother was sure her husband was suffering from sunstroke and told him he needed to wear a hat but he replied that he would never cover his head in reverence for the Lord because God's light touched his brain clear through his skull and wrapped its fingers around his thoughts until he realized the Lord Almighty had called the family to leave the farm as soon as they could pack up only their clothing because they were heading west to join the Sons of Melchizedek and practice a new way of life. This had happened to her father before and when they picked up and left they always returned because the ways of man were a disappointment no matter how godly his fair creatures – and that didn't include flies – tried to be.

When Eleanor was eight, her family joined a group of the faithful where the women were instructed to wear long dresses no matter how hot the day was and set their hair up in an up-sweep above their eyes as if an angel lifted their womanly elegance from their foreheads so they could look unto the Lord above and feel His power and know His wrath. Eleanor's mother had not been happy because Eleanor's father wanted his wife and children, including Sadie who was only two, to obey his solemn commands. Crying was considered disobedience.

Eleanor took three long sips of lemonade and continued. Something happened to Sadie. Her mother wouldn't say what. Either the baby had fallen ill or she had cried after her father commanded her to obey him but after that Sadie was gone without explanation. She asked if that was being inconsiderate and Mrs. Carlisle agreed that it most certainly was. Soon after the baby's disappearance, the family returned from the Sons of Gabriel to the family hog farm and Eleanor had to work twice as hard because the county was trying to take the land for back taxes and Eleanor's father was being charged with cruelty to animals because he'd walked away from his livestock and left the hogs and a cow to fend for themselves. The cow was caught several farms away but the hogs didn't do well because they were penned up.

As she and her mother dragged the hogs from the mud of the barnyard where they had fused with the land, the sacred land as her mother called it, Eleanor bent over and was sick from the smell. That's why she asked Mrs. Carlisle not to serve her bacon for breakfast after her guardian put a hearty plate in front of her the morning after Bob dropped her at her safe house. Mrs. Carlisle made great eggs. Her secret was a little bit of garlic powder. Eleanor told her they tasted wonderful but asked if her guardian was just a little bit afraid of the you-know-who down you-know-where who had something to do with garlic but Eleanor wasn't sure what. Mrs. Carlisle said no because her mother had been born in the south of France where everyone loves garlic and would eat it no matter what. Eleanor told her the eggs were better than a boiled potato.

"Is that all you ever got for breakfast?" and Eleanor replied un-huh, especially after her father's vision in the cornfield that sent them to live with the Children of Melchizedek.

Did Mrs. Carlisle know who Melchizedek was? Mrs. Carlisle nodded but Eleanor told her anyways. He was the angel who came to visit Lot and Lot's wife who turned to a pillar of salt for not obeying her husband, and M – she wasn't permitted to say his name too often – came to visit Lot and his family because he was going to destroy the wicked cities of Sodom and Gomorrah. Mrs. Carlisle agreed. Eleanor continued that the Children, better than the Sons because sons expect something and children just need to be seen and not heard and most of the time not seen at all, was ready to lay down their lives to destroy the wickedness of the cities, especially if they had railway stations and large office towers where wicked things happened.

"Like what?" Mrs. Carlisle asked.

Oh, just about everything wicked. I don't know everything that's wicked because I was not permitted to read or write and Bob says that's a disadvantage in this world and I have to weigh the pros with the cons, whatever they are, and just dive in and read and write and catch up from the ten years I was shut off from the world. The compound where the Children lived was lovely. There were mountains off in the distance. The summers were cooler, the winters were harder. Sadie caught sick with something and even though we prayed she went to Heaven to be with Jesus. I am frightened for her though.

"Why?" asked Mrs. Carlisle.

Eleanor stared out the kitchen window at the backyard and replied that Sadie didn't know how to read or write either and what would happen if she went to Heaven to be with Jesus and she had to sign in or fill in a job application? There'd be no one to teach her unless Eleanor showed up and she didn't want to do that because there's more to life than I thought possible. I never dreamed there were streets with cars on them. I never dreamed there were expressways and shopping malls and Happy Arches where people could walk up to the counter and choose whatever they wanted from a menu of nutritious offerings with recommended food guidelines posted on the tiled wall though no one ever bothered to read them. I want to into an office tower. I want to get on a train and go somewhere because they're like Facebook. They exist without anyone knowing they are there, just like I always thought of the Lord Almighty existing and no one realizing He was there right beside us as we worked in the fields without our hats on and only put on our scarves or caps as a sign of reverence when we came inside our houses.

"Tell me more about the Children of Melchizedek," Mrs. Carlisle said. "Did they ever speak of what they wanted to destroy?"

Eleanor didn't know. She said she had seen a map. Her father beat her for having looked upon it because he said the large paper spread upon the kitchen table late at night was a new form of scripture that would lead to the land of glory for the Children. It was pretty. There were lines all over it and I think those were highways. There were two blue snakes that met and became one snake, and her father and the other men had circled a darker area where dark lines were closer together like pieces of a quilt sewn together to make a patchwork. Momma made a patchwork quilt but she wrapped Sadie in it as she wept and we set Sadie in the Earth and my father screamed that his child's death was the work of man and I was frightened because I knew he would beat me if I even thought out the map and all its lines. But now that I have put it all behind me I want to know what the work of Man is. I want to imagine that those blue snakes are rivers and the dark patchwork is made of streets just like this one. I want to learn to read the names on the map so I can remember what it is my father and his brethren want to destroy to pull down the works of Man before the Lord Almighty.

Mrs. Carlisle asked Eleanor if she would like to take a train trip on her next day off and Eleanor was very happy replying that there had been cars and trucks and once when her family was still a family and they were driving along the highway and trying to ignore people in the other cars who stared at them because they mistook them for you-know-who down you-know-where I looked up and above me, there was a long silver train with windows moving faster than a bird chasing a fly on a summer morning, and I asked what it was and before my father could hush her words my mother said it was a train. Not just any train but a passenger train and it was heading to the city. It was full of people who were reading newspapers or books or just minding their own business and admiring the scenery as they rolled past it and they were calm. That's when my father pulled the car to the side of the road and beat my mother in a ditch. I cried but I told myself that someday I would be one of those people on a train.

So three days later Mrs. Carlisle woke me earlier than usual and made me garlic eggs and we got in her car and went where she said it was downtown, but not you-know-where down. The light was reflecting off the glass of tall buildings. The street was a rainbow I had seen once on the creek at the edge of our hog farm, and I hurried to keep up with Mrs. Carlisle who stood in line and bought two pieces of cardboard and called them tickets from a woman who sat behind glass. I heard voices like angels speaking to me from the air and then Mrs. Carlisle took my hand and led me to the top of a staircase with a number in lights on a sign at the top.

That's when I saw my father and his friends. They used to say only sinners ride on trains. They are sinners because they stare out their windows and look at all the poor folk and don't do nothing for them. How could they? They were traveling. Sinners have to go somewhere. That's why they ride the train.

He saw me. He saw me like he'd seen a vision and he stared at me. I wanted to call to him but Bob said I mustn't have anything to do with him again and I was frightened because I didn't want him to beat me anymore, not there, not then. And as we descended the steps I could see the train. It was silver and had dark windows that were staring with mystery and just as Mrs. Carlisle and I were about to grab hold of long metal handles and step up to the train my father grabbed me by the arm so tight it hurt and raised a hand to strike me but his palm never touched me because the hand of the Lord came down as if it was smoting a fly against a wall and the station exploded all around me. I said don't to him but he wouldn't listen so I pulled away and he called after me, but I ran as hard as I could to the far end of the train and Mrs. Carlisle leaned out from the top of the steps and called my name but my father shouted Thy Will Be Done and Mrs. Carlisle and my father disappeared and I got knocked to the ground as if it was the hand of the Lord and everything was smitten if that's the word for being smote and I tried to say don't but nothing would leave my lips except blood and blood is holy so I was certain the Lord was there among us because the train rained down on me in pieces of metal and I had to love the Lord because there was no other choice that I still wanted to say don't.

A Short Film About Seagulls
(shortlisted Fish Flash Fiction Prize)

By the end of September, the days were still as warm as they'd been in July with the only difference being the deserted streets and the shuttered cottages that reminded me how time passes and leaves its silences behind.

We'd been residents since May.

She was up early every morning, long before I was awake.

She'd disappear down the beach with her camera and tripod, her Capri's darkened where the waves touched her shins above the frayed cuffs and the wind making her hair wild as if she spent time in a lover's arms.

Even in rough weather, when the sea turned grey and the tidelines shifted precariously toward the dunes that separated the cottage from the sound, she'd return by ten, her head and back sandy, saying it had been tough to get the shots she wanted.

As I put my manuscripts in cartons and wove the flaps together the way someone might have clasped her hand, I realized I had failed to script my own life, and having given up being a character, was out of the picture.

I pressed the trigger.

The camera was empty. The feed sprockets whirred. Frame by frame, nothing had captured the illusions.

Gulls didn't follow her the way she said they did, but one hovered motionless over the cottage deck, its wings spread, pages in the middle of a story. That's when I saw him kiss her goodbye. That's how this film ends.

Worldly Goods
(The Song Between Our Stars)

The storage facility was open twenty-four hours a day because physicians kept their records in the padlocked cells that reminded me of prisons I'd seen on television. Two in the morning had seemed a good idea when I began. I didn't want to be alone but the longer I shifted and hauled my late aunt Shirley's left me, the more exhausted I felt and the more I was overcome by a feeling of disturbing the dead.

My aunt and I had never been close but I inherited her worldly goods. My mother often admitted she found her sister Shirley overbearing. My aunt insisted on being the keeper of my grandparent's belongings. She scooped up everything and hoarded it. When Shirley died it all went into storage. There was the sofa with traces of lily of the valley perfume that remained from Gran's afternoon naps.

As I struggled to shift a dresser, I realized hell is keeping other people's possessions long after they are dead. Shirley locked her mother away in the twelve-by-ten vault, entombing her like a Pharaoh for ruining her future.

Shirley never married and blamed my grandmother for chasing away suitors. I sat down in an overstuffed easy chair from the Thirties and wondered if I should be unpacking the dead and their troubles.

I closed my eyes and moved through the rooms of my grandmother's house. It had been a happy place for me. I remembered the things that weren't there – the claw-foot bathtub, the cast iron kitchen sink draining board.

I thought it would be nice to surprise my Mom with a photograph of the three of them. They were standing beside a lake, smiling, if I remembered the picture correctly. Happiness. A rare moment lost in time

I had been through dresser drawers and cedar chests and poked among the layers of two lives. I was ready to give up when I found what I was looking for in the buffet that still held my grandmother's silverware, tarnished from years in the dark stillness. I held the photo to the light.

They weren't as I remembered them.

Shirley was scowling at my grandmother. My mother was the only one smiling. The past hadn't been worth the trouble of finding it.

Dawn was coming.

I had to put everything back where it had been, including the ghosts. They cannot handle a new day and they fade the moment they are touched by sunlight.

The Brothers

The Galle-Gamache brothers were into Christmas trees. I'd help drive loads down to the city and sell them to suckers for five times the price just before Christmas. Everyone in the north works an angle. We have to if we're going to keep afloat. The favorites are contraband tobacco, unexcised liquor from the reserves, and Christmas trees from Crown Land. There is so much Crown Land nobody misses them.

The brothers were both called Hal though they had different names. Henry Hal was the more erudite of the two, haughty but people believed him. He had what I'd call "nurture." He could sell a pipe cleaner to someone desperate enough on Christmas Eve. The other brother was Harold Hal. He was a "nature" man. He knew his way around the bush and could drag ten to fifteen medium-sized trees out in one trip. He was an expert on snowshoes. Harold Hal could sleep rough. His unkempt beard made him fearsome. The Ministry of Natural Resources men stayed clear of him even when he was hunting out of season or hauling pine and fir saplings to his truck.

The brothers heard the MNR replanted the far side of Skid Lake about five years ago after a burn-off. The trees would be the right size. Skid is on the map but a map isn't useful because no one ever goes there. As they were crossing, the lake the ice broke beneath Harold. The air was warm but the water was frigid and Harold refused to let go of his load or kick off his boots and snowshoes. He disappeared. Henry couldn't swim. He kept jabbing a tree into the hole hoping Harold would come up and grab it.

There was no way Henry could tell the cops what had happened. He'd be charged with deforesting Crown Land. He drove his load south as if nothing had gone wrong.

I haven't seen Henry since last summer. I was picking blueberries. Henry had on scuba gear and clutched a fistful of flowers. He dove into Skid, chased by a water moccasin, but not before shouting he'd bring Hal back to life.

Toothbrush (Hash Journal)

If a lie is different from a secret I will never tell where the rabbit went because when I was four I learned to brush my teeth and knew I was unhappy but had no way of going to a happy place. My family was not the problem. My parents were loving, my grandparents doting. But the boy across the street came into my garden and hit me until I cried.

He was six. His name was Leslie Yawnton and he beat me up because he said I was a little liar who told stories.

One morning on television I saw a man in a rocket fly into the sky.

The voice on the television said, "Possibilities are now as vast as our imaginations." I asked my mother what imagination was.

"Think of pictures in your mind. Think of faraway places," she said.

"Where is the man in the rocket going?"

"Wherever our imaginations take us."

"Do I have an imagination?"

"Yes, dear, you do, though sometimes you have too much."

"Like when you don't believe me if I tell you Leslie hit me?"

She didn't answer. Maybe she wanted to believe me, but she never caught Leslie in the act of sitting on top of me and hitting me repeatedly in the face.

The day I saw the rocket man, Leslie appeared in my garden. He had climbed over the fence or undone the gate. I told him I had seen a man go up into the sky and fly among the stars.

Leslie said I was lying and kept punching me in the head.

In a puff of smoke, the spaceman in a white helmet and silver suit who carried his air in a box made me imagine I could go somewhere else. Leslie grabbed me in a chokehold.

"You are a dirty little liar who tells stories."

He slapped me until I couldn't fight back the tears, insisting there was no one in the sky and if anyone went there they would fall down and die. I "needed my mouth washed out."

My grandmother had given me a red toothbrush with a round head and white bristles and if I stood on a wooden stool my father built so I could see myself in the bathroom mirror I could watch my mouth froth with every up and down stroke though I preferred the back and forth motion of the bristles on my teeth. The more Leslie hit me, the longer I wanted to clean my mouth.

Leslie's mother was the social doyenne of the street. She would tell all the mothers in the neighborhood that her son was a perfect angel when they gathered at the Yawnton house for afternoon coffee parties. She told the other mothers I was disturbed.

I knew a secret about their house. Beneath the back bedroom was a crawl space with a dirt floor where Leslie's father kept old lumber. Leslie called it his gold mine and had once dragged me in there by the hair to beat me up.

The day after the rocket man's flight, when Leslie thought I had surrendered, he'd tried to enter his house but his mother was asleep and wouldn't answer the door. I followed him to his backyard and hid in the bushes until he vanished into the crawl space where he beat the dirt with a spade. When I was certain he'd gone in too far to catch me, I shut the door and snapped the padlock in the latch. Then I went home and brushed my teeth because I knew I would have to lie if anyone asked where Leslie had gone.

The red plastic handle in my hand foamed with white froth. The taste of mint from Dr. Soane's Dental Cream for Children made my teeth whiter with every stroke until I was certain they shone like the rocket man's helmet as he climbed into his tiny room and a man in a white coat handed him his box of air so he could breathe when he touched the stars.

TOOTHBRUSH

By the next evening, Leslie's mother was frantic. She appeared at our door just after I had been put to bed. I heard her downstairs weeping and asking if anyone had seen Leslie.

"He said he was going out to play with your son, that dirty little liar of yours."

My mother came into my room and asked if I knew where Leslie had gone.

I said I had. Leslie had gone someplace to find happiness but I could not imagine where.

"Try harder," my mother said.

I shut my eyes and pictured a morning in my garden. The sun was shining. A grey rabbit hopped across the lawn and made a "Shush" with its forefoot then waved "So long!"

Auntie

"Don't you feel breezy today?" she'd ask as she laughed.

Auntie never said where she was from or which side of the family she belonged to, but she loved to dance, alone or with a partner, and tried to teach us every step she knew. Her accent shifted from day to day depending on what she decided to cook for us, and she loved to cook as much as we loved eating what she prepared. We couldn't remember when she moved in or if she ever said she'd move out.

In the beginning, Auntie's shadow resembled a pencil but as she grew older she became, as one family member put it, more upholstered. We brought her to the beach one July afternoon and took turns sitting in the shade she cast.

We asked if she had ever been in love and she answered, "Of course, many times in many places but now she loved us all equally," which was both sad and reassuring because all of us wanted to be Auntie's favorite.

We returned one evening from a long bicycle ride. When we left, Auntie had been on the porch to wave goodbye, but by dusk, she wasn't there to greet us. Mother was upstairs weeping at Auntie's bedside, and we asked what had happened. Someone so great, so full of love would surely have lived forever.

Our disbelief was strong. We all wanted to wish her back to life. Moonlight was flooding in the window of our room and we were in awe when the curtains rustled and bulged and we agreed Auntie was hiding behind them, beckoning us to dance.

Rust

Our mother purchased a new two-door car that was gold and had plaid seats. We'd never had a vehicle where the front seats flipped forward so we could climb in the back. The dealer said it was 'sporty.' We reveled in the idea that our mother could put her foot down, gun the motor, and leave the world in our dust.

We decided to take a long, motor vacation across the country. Our father did most of the driving because he wanted to see how fast he could go and not get caught by a speed trap.

Our mother commanded the front passenger seat and assumed the role of disciplinarian and navigator with "Triptychs" from the Motor League that were narrow flipbooks that outlined our route and pointed out important sites along the way. We sat in the back and pretended not to notice.

The car was also our first automobile to have a radio in the dashboard. Before we bought the new, gold car our parents had driven clunkers that were as heavy as tanks because they had been made just after the war by factories that produced armored vehicles. The old cars had all the qualities of a tank except the turret.

The addition of the radio was a nod to comfort, although the windows had to be rolled down by hand in the front seats and in the back, they popped open on small, black snap hinges. Mother said power windows were an unnecessary expense. Rolling built muscles.

"Hey, do you want to see me outrun our shadow?" our father asked late one day when we had been tied up in a traffic jam caused by construction and were racing to make our motel reservation.

He put his foot on the accelerator.

We raced past a policeman and waved. Instead of chasing us down and pulling us over for a ticket, he waved back.

As we unloaded our bags and climbed up to our room in the gallery of the motel, we stared over the rail at our new car and admired its lines. Nothing, we agreed, could catch it. It was sleek. We agreed it could outrun everything including time.

The next morning when we rose early because my father was determined to get on the road before the highway jammed up again, we dragged our suitcases out of our room and looked down on our new car. It had been cool during the night. The car was covered in dew. The inside of the windshield looked like an aquarium. We argued over what we would write on the windows when we climbed in.

That's when my father found the first problem. The flaw was not in the engine. It had been manufactured in Detroit, he told us.

The flaw was a spot of rust on the rear passenger side panel.

My mother stood and looked at it with him.

They both tried to rub it off. The paint had bubbled and the metal had turned reddish-brown.

"It is just going to get worse," they said in unison, looking at each other.

"It is still under warranty," mother said.

"It is going to get bigger," father replied. "It must have happened when we drove through the gravel patch in the roadwork yesterday. Gravel is rough on paint jobs, especially new ones."

We could tell they were worried.

The further we got from home, the more we kept pulling over in picnic areas to inspect the damage. It was getting worse.

It reminded us of ringworm which we had caught from playing in a barnyard with some piglets, or worse, a patch of psoriasis.

When we asked our mother if the car had psoriasis she said, "No, but the patch on the rear panel," that now spread all the way to the back bumper and had begun to populate on the chrome "was just like that, only cars aren't human. They don't have progressive skin diseases."

The problem spread from the paint to the chrome and got worse whenever we lost a radio signal. It was as if the mod-gold color was held on the body of the vehicle by waves or signals. We kept insisting our mother dial around for a station.

"There's nothing on the radio."

"Keep looking!"

By the time we reached the seashore and could smell the salt air but the car was beginning to vanish. The frame was crumbling but the windows were intact. The beach, we told our father, was good for the car.

"There are lots of Top 40 stations on the radio."

"No," he said, "the salt air is making the problem worse. We're going to have to head to higher ground."

The ocean was fun for us but we could see what our father saw – the car was dissolving. We knew he was worried we might not get home.

We'd have to walk all the way, through the construction and dust and rain and heat on the shoulder of the road, lugging our suitcases in one hand and using the other hand for balance.

As we drove home, we noticed the car was not the only thing that was succumbing to the oxidization of metal, as our father put it. Entire towns were beginning to rust.

At first, the decay was not entirely noticeable. The houses and churches were white clapboard. But when we reached the factory cities, the places where we'd seen workers filing out of factories at the end of their shifts were being eaten by rust.

We paused at a pull-off and heard the sound of rust chewing metal.

Had we caused it?

Perhaps.

Maybe in outrunning our shadow, which we were sure we had when we started out, we had left a trail not of dust but of rust. We could see bridges being eaten away as we crossed them and the cars behind plunging into the abyss of deep rivers where they dissolved as they were swept away.

The Trailer
(London Independent Short Story Prize finalist)

He was certain he had lived his life before. His performance in this life, the still images other people would mistake for memories, boiled down to a handful of brief scenes where his best acting gave a taste of what the feature film would be. There were moments he felt Oscar-worthy and instances when the drama of life was too powerful to be contained in a trailer for the coming-to a theatre-near-you blockbuster.

Sonorous voice intones, "This is the story of a man in search of love who finds instead…"

Between those short, punctuated bursts of reality cut together by the marketing department, he couldn't remember his life. There had to be more to it, but production had wrapped ages ago.

He bought himself a trailer when he quit university and parked it deep in the bush. His only visitors were deer and bears. The bears tried the windows when they thought he wasn't home. When they stood on their hind legs they reminded him of his aunts who found his remote location and peered in the windows.

"Couldn't you do something better with your life?" they asked.

The full-length feature would connect all the scenes of dramatic tension – such as the time he ran from his girlfriend when she stood with her eyes closed and her lips puckered as moths circled the light fixture on her front porch. Her arms were open in a bear hug to hold him forever until her jaws clamped around his face and tore off his identity.

If he hadn't seen the end that was cut from the trailer, he wouldn't have gotten away. He wouldn't have stopped to bend down and weep, breathless from running five blocks from her house, and wonder where his ball cap fell off, and who was wearing it now.

Arums (Lothlarien Review)

"If I had arms like an octopus I'd wrap them all around you and give you a big birthday hug," Aunt Harriet wrote on the pink card with oversized arum lilies on the front and a poem inside that rhymed "a friend so kind" with "you in mind." She was large and her kisses were wet as oceans.

When Harriet passed only days after the card arrived, his mother canceled his party for the second year – he'd had chickenpox when he was seven – and packed him in the car.

"Nothing is fair," she told him, "not life, not death, not even love, and of those three life death happen anyways and love was the most difficult because it is hard to hold onto."

It rained all the way south. Spring was barely in bloom and the car windows fogged. His mother refused to drive with the radio on but the beat of the wipers and the steady thread of boredom put him to sleep.

When they arrived, Aunt Thelma had turned the mattress in Harriet's room for them, and when they woke and his mother adjusted his suit she insisted he wear his clip-on bow tie because all the men in the family wear them.

Aunt Harriet lay in her box in the living room window, the bier embellished with arrangements of arum lilies. Their open mouths made the flowers appear to gasp or cry out for help. The rose scent of perfumed women and the headiness of the flowers in the fierce humidity made him think he was wrapped in a dog's panting.

A bald man, heavyset with his shirt buttons pulling, stood next to him as he stared at his aunt in her stillness.

"I'm your Uncle Grant. Thelma and Harriet's brother. I don't think we've met."

The boy said nothing.

"Your Mom's raising you. She's a brave woman. They're brave women. Has anyone given you had the talk yet? I want to get to know you, teach you how to tie a bow tie like mine, and tell you where to hold your hands on the steering wheel when you get pulled over."

The boy didn't understand. He'd watched his mother drive. He turned and went outside to the porch.

In the grey daylight, the houses in their stiff front faces looked alike, but what made each one different was the paint on their clapboard, some of it peeling, some blue, some yellow. He leaned over the porch railing.

In the flower bed directly below, a single white lily had bloomed, its mouth open to the sky as if it wanted to suck down the clouds by catching raindrops to quench its thirst so he and his mother could go home.

He went down the steps and tried to snap the stem, but the shaft was supple. It bent in his hands. The sinews held fast. The flower drooped. He knelt and using his pocket knife, cut through the stalk, mangling it with each pass of the dull blade. He would give the flower to Harriet, lay it beside her in her box, and write a small card that said, "You in mind."

The women in the kitchen didn't see him tear the bottom off Harriet's last shopping list or notice as he laid the arum beside his aunt. He wanted her to know he loved her though she had always been far away and ruined his birthday.

He heard his uncle calling out, almost in a shout so everyone could hear, "Where's that boy?"

Grant grabbed him by the shoulder and took him out to the porch and made him look over the railing at the lily stub.

"Why did you take your aunt's last flower? She grew lilies. That was her last. She poured her love into them, every year kneeling close to the earth and saying she thought she heard angels there. The last lily was her way of saying goodbye to everyone, and you've ruined it. You got mud in her coffin. What were you thinking?"

He didn't know what to say. He wanted to cry.

He ran upstairs to his aunt's room where he and his mother slept and buried his face in the pillow until everything was dark with a terrible lightlessness that pricked him with shame and emptiness from the weight on his shoulders down to his stomach.

His aunt had so many arms, so many ways of reaching out and drawing people to her, and the void he saw as he pressed his face to the pillow resembled ink, and he thought he would ask her forgiveness by writing a story about her, perhaps with the title "You In Mind," and the ink was right before his eyes.

Sweet Things

Karla and Millicent walked into Melnyk's Drugstore one Saturday afternoon in July for some candy and before they were able to leave both were convinced they were going to hell. The afternoon was a slow and blazing day and the sidewalks shimmered in the heat where spats of grey chewing gum around the pharmacy's entrance stuck to the soles of the girls' shoes if they stood more than a quick step in one spot. Most of the customers were out of town, or cutting their lawns, or picnicking down at the waterfront, and Doug Melnyk, who had known both the girls since they were toddlers, decided to leave the prescription counter and sit behind the cash in case someone came in to buy a newspaper or made a grab for the till.

The bell over the door rattled a few notes. Karla swung the door back and forth and listened as they rattled. The greeting chimes were a pleasant sound she'd always loved. Melnyk stood up to greet them.

The girls said nothing.

He watched as they moved up and down the aisles, stopping to sample the tester bottles of perfume or pry open the caps of shampoos to smell the fragrance.

Karla leaned into Millicent and whispered in her ear before they approached the druggist, and the girls elbowed each other to see who would speak first.

"Where is your ice cream freezer, the one with the metal doors on top?" Karla asked.

"Well girls, the freezer mechanism broke. Worst time of year it could have clunked out on me. This is popsicle season.

I have Lifesavers and chocolate bars although I wouldn't say it's chocolate weather."

"What is a Baby Ruth?" Millicent asked.

"It has chocolate and peanuts and some sort of nougat. People think it's named after the baseball player, but I read up on it and it got called that for Grover Cleveland's daughter who died of diphtheria almost twenty years before it was invented."

"Yuck," said Karla, making a face. "Diphtheria? Will I get it from the candy bar?"

Melnyk smiled. "No. It has almost been eradicated. My grandmother had it when she was a girl and almost died, and right around the time Ruth Cleveland died of it. It used to carry off the elderly and young ones just like you two. People would catch it in the summer. They'd burn up from it, I guess like they'd been tossed on a fire."

The counter was set on a high platform, and Melnyk stared down at Millicent who had taken two bars off the rack and slipped them into the back band of her blue jeans.

"You know, Millie, that's stealing."

"I didn't steal anything."

"Really?"

"Cross my heart and hope to die."

"Well, in that case, I'd wager you are going to come down with diphtheria sometime soon," the pharmacist said. The color drained from Millicent's face. She turned to Karla. "You can put them back."

"You told me it would be easy!" Millicent shouted at her friend. While the thief and the owner were distracted, Karla pocketed her own handful of bars off the rack.

'Run!" she shouted.

"Not so fast," said Melnyk as he reached under the counter and a button buzzed and the door with the pleasant bells locked as if by magic. The girls tugged on the doorknob but it wouldn't open. Millicent began to cry and pound her fist on the frame. She turned to Karla and shook her, and Karla's loot dropped to the floor.

"Do you know what diphtheria does?" asked the druggist. "It sorts the good from the bad. The good who die go to heaven where they get to eat all the chocolate bars they want. The bad burn up in fevers and go to hell where their Baby Ruth bars melt into puddles as if they were left in a car with the windows rolled up. I think you should put the bars back."

Karla looked up at Melnyk. His white coat with his name embroidered on the side without a pocket was unbuttoned and he had a strawberry or rhubarb stain on the front of his shirt. "No, you go to hell."

The druggist stared at the two girls, especially Millicent, and she felt his eyes burning her soul. Tears welled up in her eyes. "It's hotter than hell out there," he said. "Chocolate never does well in the heat. It turns liquid and melts into a horrible mess. So do people who go to hell. Hell has no time, and I don't have all the time in the world, so we'll just wait here for your folks to come and find you."

He reached up to the air conditioning unit over the door, flipped the switch off then sat back down in his chair as the store grew as warm as an oven in the afternoon stillness. The girls stood in the grip of the angry sun as it flowed through the panel the door where the store's name was painted in reverse letters like a curse in a mystical script, and the heat melted everything it touched including their last shred of nerve.

Karla finally broke. "Did Grover Cleveland's daughter go to hell?"

"I don't think so. I don't think she was even caught stealing candy bars, at least not the ones named after her."

Aces

My brother and I were too young to have been reading about the exploits of the World War One fighter ace, Billy Bishop. The flier had been of our grandfather's generation, and though the old man never spoke about his own experiences in the trenches, he was incessant about Bishop who he considered a hero.

The famous aviator had risen before dawn on the final morning of his posting to a squadron at the front. Grandpa would point a finger on his left hand at us – he'd lost most of his right hand in the war and wouldn't talk about how had only a thumb and index finger remaining – and say, "Boys, bravery is doing what you don't need to do. Billy Bishop didn't need to get up in the darkest hour that day. He was going back to Blighty at eleven. But instead, he climbed into his cockpit and as the sun came up over the front, he shot up a German aerodrome and registered five kills before calling it a day."

We asked him if he'd seen Billy Bishop during the war. Grandpa thought for a moment. His eyes darted back and forth. In his mind he was somewhere else, someplace he had not sorted out in his thoughts. Then he nodded. Yes. He'd seen the famous flier. He'd looked up one clear spring morning and witnessed a dogfight above him. That was all the old man would say.

I found a book in the local library. I had just begun to read. My brother would listen as I struggled with the words. Bishop's autobiography was too old for me, but my brother and I marveled at the passage where the ace recounted how wanted to fly before the war began and built an airplane out of junk wood and orange crates and attempted to glide it off the slanted roof of his boyhood home. We decided we could do the same.

Bishop was lucky. He only broke his leg. In photographs, the great ace is pictured leaning on the wing of his Nieuport scout, and the walking stick he required is either settled on the silver wing or leaned against the fuselage. The week our parents were away in New York, my brother and I figured out how to climb the tree outside our bedroom window, and with a series of ropes hoisted lumber we found by the creek and in the laneway that ran behind the houses on our street.

The war had left our grandfather monodextrous and deaf so the old man was none the wiser to the hammering on the roof. When we'd come inside for dinner, he'd ask my brother and me if we were behaving ourselves and remind us not to stray too far from home.

As our airplane neared completion, my brother went into our mother's dresser drawer and found a yellow swim cap with rubber daisies garlanding the crown and the swim goggles she'd purchased with the intention of doing lengths at the local YWCA though she never found the time. I wanted my brother to turn the cap inside out when he flew – he had demanded to be the first to have a go and said that if he couldn't be Billy Bishop he'd be Wilbur Wright to my Orville, though neither of us was sure who had been the first to fly and which one had died when their 'Kittyhawk' crashed. I was to give the aircraft its power by pushing it over the shingles and past the eavestrough.

Our grandfather had a habit of getting up in the night and passing our door on the way to the bathroom, and on his return, he'd look in our room and check to make sure we were asleep. We thought we'd timed his trips according to how many cups of tea he'd had before bed, but that night we got it wrong. The sight of our empty beds panicked him.

He'd told us that empty bunks in the Officer's dugouts signaled who had been killed or missing in action.

He saw our bedroom window open with the cool night air playing in the curtains. My brother had torn his hockey pajamas on a twig that protruded from the tree we used to access the roof, and when Grandpa went to the window he saw my brother fly past as our contraption dove nose-first into the yard. It smashed a wing against the tree on its way down and ejected from the broken wicker lawn chair we'd cut down for a seat.

By the time I scrambled down the tree, my grandfather was already bent over my motionless brother who had a strange smile on his face, not of happiness but of calm.

The old guy was weeping.

He kept asking why. He looked at me with a terrifying and accusatory intensity and muttered something about looking after the little guy and what on earth was I thinking.

Then he began to shake. He crouched in a ball next to my brother and shook.

The sun was coming up on the late summer morning but in the dewy air, I could see my breath. The grass glistened.

The yard was littered with broken lumber and a blue, white, and red roundel we'd painted on a drop cloth we'd found in the garage and wrapped around one of the wings. My brother lay at an awkward angle and the strap of the swim goggles cut into the crown of rubber daisies. He hadn't listened when I told him to turn the swim cap inside out so he would look like a real ace.

The Boiling Point (A Chronicle of Magpies)

Gwen stared out the window at the blizzard and waited for the courier to come with Maggie's precious metformin pills. She thought about the trail dogs that once ran to deliver medicine to remote communities such as hers and was reminded of the name of the first encyclopedist. Iditarod. Diderot.

Moving here from the city had been Dave's idea. The telephone company needed linemen, and they offered to double his pay.

Thin wires of conversation stretched along the old logging roads and hydro clear cuts. She had been playing tin-can telephone with Mags on a morning like this when she received word that Dave had slipped and fallen from a repeater station early the night before. He had lain in the snow through long lonely hours, his cellphone useless because he had shut down the tower to repair it. The weather gradually crept inside him, leaving a starry patch among the snow-laden pines and silence on his phone.

One very cold day when Gwen was eight, her mother put a pot on the stove to boil. She called the girls into the kitchen as steam clouds rose. "Open the back door!" she exclaimed. "I'm going to show you a miracle!" With the door wide open, Gwen had felt the deep chill wrap its arms around her. Her mother took the pot and flung the contents into the air. In an instant, the scalding liquid became snow.

Mags walked into the kitchen in her sleepers. Her face was grey, and her forehead was covered in beads of cold sweat. The mother and daughter exchanged glances that betrayed the fact that both knew, almost instinctively, that the situation was growing direr by the minute.

A pot of hot water that Gwen had put on for tea was mumbling on the stove.

"Let me show you something," Gwen said, trying to cheer her child. She grabbed the pot from the burner and set it momentarily on the countertop beside the kitchen door. With a push, she was able to force the door over the newly stacked snow that tried to bar her inside the house. Mags approached cautiously as Gwen picked up the pot of steaming water.

"Watch," she said to the child. "Mommy is going to make magic." The air, as she breathed in, hardened inside her nose to the point that she could almost feel her head crack. She flung the water into the air above the small porch, and instantly it became a reeling cloud of steam.

Mags gasped and Gwen dropped the pot of water as Dave's pale shadow appeared in the sudden whir of snowflakes, his hands empty and reaching out to them.

The Old Man (Fictive Dream)

There had been so many fierce tropical storms that year the National Hurricane Center exhausted its alphabetical list of names and by early September they were christening category fives with a new sequence of ABCs. We were living on the coast when Alex passed through after Walter. My wife, kids, and I took refuge in a bedroom closet on the second floor at the back of the house. We believed we were safe until a pine tree crashed through the roof, crushing our bed and dresser, and stranding us for three days high above the ground with the tidal surge swirling around the foundations of our house.

Determined not to get caught on low ground again, we relocated twenty miles inland where we thought we were safe.

But Douglas was different.

The water rose twenty feet above sea level in a matter of hours, and when I put my eye to a knothole in the plywood on the front window I saw waves coursing over our lawn and could smell the salt in it.

We spent the night in the crawl space of the attic. If the water had been six inches higher, we would have drowned as we sheltered in place. Douglas was our last warning. We should have evacuated when we had the chance. The first arm of wind ripped off the shingles and the next arm tore at the decking of the roof. Our children were screaming but the gale force wind drowned out their cries.

Then silence.

It wasn't the silence of the storm's eye. That had long passed.

It was the absence of sound that might have greeted Noah when he sent forth the raven from his ark. I pried open the front door. The neighborhood was gone. A heap of broken lumber and the sign for a gas station a mile down the highway was floating in a foot of water where the house across the street once stood.

And there was a man on our front lawn.

He faced down. His arms appeared to be clutching something that had been torn from his embrace. He was still wearing his undershirt. I waded out and covered the lower half of his body with a sheet of shingles and sat down at the edge of what had been our porch to wait for rescuers to arrive.

My wife called me to come in. I told her to go back in the house. I didn't know what else to say. I didn't want her to see the body.

I had switched off the electricity and gas before Douglas hit, but some had not done so. A hydro wire sparked from the one pole left standing on the block. Our rental house was the only structure left standing. We'd been lucky.

People lived here. It wasn't fair this should happen to them. It wasn't fair that month after month, year after year, storms kept coming and grew more intense every time they struck.

And what could I do about the man – and old man from the look of him –

sprawled where the storm surge had carried him, perhaps sweeping him from the arms of his wife as they lay together in bed, hoping to ride out the worst of it or clutching his dog, the frightened animal fighting so hard for life it abandoned the old man in his time of need. Or maybe he had fallen from the sky as the eye of the hurricane picked him up and dropped him where he lay. I have heard stories of angels falling from Heaven. They are battered from the wrath of the sky, just like the old man on the lawn. And though I do not believe angels fall unless they are torn from the kingdom of clouds during hurricanes, I accept they can be carried twenty miles inland in the grip of a storm surge.

I wanted to feel for him. I wanted to sit down and weep beside his body and ask why he had let go of what he once held. I wanted to know his name. I wanted him to ask him about his life, how he worked for years, built his own world, did good or bad – neither mattered now – and saw everything he knew and loved shattered in a single night.

Had he been washed all this way inland from the coast? Had he been someone local whose final journey was short? The longer he lay there, motionless and clutching at what he lost, the more he blended with the debris and I was angry at myself for having grown inured to calamity and numb to the consequences of living so recklessly in the world

He was bald and his grey hair was wild and tufted from having been tossed in the surge. He had at least two days of stubble on his face. Had he spent his final hour preparing a futile defense against the blast? Who was he? Someone's husband? A family's father just like me or a grandfather, or the elderly uncle who decided to be brave and ride it out?

Both he and I were fools for believing we could stand our ground instead of running for safety. Perhaps he had no means to run or was confused and didn't know where to go if he did head for safety. We both believed in the brave myth of 'shelter in place.' But bravery means nothing to a hurricane. It does not hear our taunts or our shouts or even our anguished cries when we realize we miscalculated our odds of survival.

And soon there would be Edward, after that Felix, and the whiplash of George.

I wondered where I would have ended up had I been in his place with no fight left in my body or soul and let myself become a nameless traveler in the drift and debris with no idea where or when I would arrive at the journey's end and with no one to greet me there and no way for me to call to them if they were and only silence to tell them who I was.

Happy (Finding the Birds)

My wife and I compete to see who can do the best at the crossword every morning over breakfast. We have two subscriptions to the same newspaper. Breakfast is coffee and a kind of high noon showdown over the breakfast table. Some couples say too little to each other as they begin their days. We say too much. The crosswords are not necessarily crosswords, but they are pointed, barbed, and at times meant to sting, at least in our intonations. I like to think that the morning crossword is a way to get our brains going for the day.

I and my wife were arguing about the word "*psithurism*," a Greek word meaning "the sound of wind through trees."

The word sounds like zither which, perhaps, is a great-grandchild of the Aeolian harp, a stringed instrument played by the wind. I tried to tell her when the word came up that I once lived on the top floor of an apartment building on the Detroit River.

My building's roof terrace was surrounded by an aluminum rail, but the uprights weren't locked down properly and when a storm came up, my bedroom was like the inside of a guitar, a sound box, that only served to amplify the music of the balustrade. But before I could even get to the part of the story where I talked about the wind, she shushed me. She never even let me get to the part where the superintendent wanted to have me locked up for wrapping yellow nylon cord around each upright because I said the railing played music all night. That's when the building management company sealed off the roof to tenant access. *P-S-I-T-H-U-R-I-S-M.*

First, she said, "Shut up." That was harsher than usual because on a good day she would put her index finger to her lips like a librarian and on a bad day, she would say, "Be quiet," in a scolding voice. She added, "I don't know why you invent words like that," and as if to assert her superiority had to suffix that statement with her inability to fathom that anyone could attribute any odd piece of jargon to the Greeks because none of the ancient ones were still alive to say otherwise. "That's why we don't bother with ancient Greek words today unless we really need them. And we don't."

So I said, "Like what?" and she answered, "the philosophy of happiness, *eudaimonia*. Fourteen down. There. I just gave you one."

"We don't think much about happiness. And I already had that, for your information. In fact, our age seems to think that happiness is an overrated experience."

I was not going to give her the pleasure of winning the point. I'm a bastard first thing in the morning and I will argue a point to death just for the sake of the battle. Happiness is a war that is easy to start and even easier to lose.

She stared at me over her reading glasses.

"Other couples argue about important things – money, children, relatives, the division of chores, shopping, the color of walls and carpet, places to vacation. They argue about responsibilities," she said. "Every damned morning you're arguing philology."

"Well," I said, to get her goat, "you're the Classics scholar. Why don't we argue about happiness? You, of all people, should know these Greek words backward and forwards, and before you say no to the proposition that happiness is overrated here's why. As a Philosophy professor, I can posit that two academics should never marry. If two parties argue about happiness ad infinitum there can be no reasonable opportunity for them to experience happiness, at least not in a broad, extended sense, and ipso facto at least one should, by virtue of the nature of debate, come out on top. The winner is happy. Maybe not the loser, but at least one person achieves a state of *eudaimonia*. Therefore, two academics can never be happy arguing the nature of happiness."

I felt as if I had just won the point when she began to cry.

She looked at me through her tears.

"You're so bloody competitive and cerebral, too. A relationship, happy or otherwise, isn't about who wins or loses."

"Is it about how one plays the game?" I asked.

That made her angry.

"There *is* no damned game. Don't you realize that? It is hell living with you. You're an asshole who thinks he knows more than me yet when it comes to the Greeks you bloody well don't."

"That's because I'm an epistemologist, not some toss-off Socratic sphinx who does nothing but ask people questions until they get one right and knock off the bugger on the outskirts of Thebes, or whatever place it was where Oedipus had it out with the quizmaster creature."

Then she went silent. She grabbed my copy of the crossword from my hands and wrote in *psithurism* with her ballpoint.

"There," she said, "you win. Happy are we?"

I had read somewhere in one of those relaxation therapy magazines I picked up in a dentist's waiting room that a smile changes the whole *ethos* of a room. *Ethos.* That's a word she'd love. The article stated that if one person smiled at another, not only would the other person smile back as a kind of *phatic* response from the Greek *phatos* meaning "spoken" but the resultant unspoken bond forged between the smiler and the smilee would, at that moment, precipitate a change not only smilee but in the smiler who would feel joy and happiness from initiating the gesture.

And I didn't want to lose, at least not on her terms where she claimed I won and then sulked about it, because that's a form of defeat, and I know it is a form of defeat because she got her own way by belittling me with her own expression of tragic downfall that evoked a catharsis in me. Right out of Aristotle's *Poetics*. She wins. I lose.

I hate losing. Fear of losing is the plague of males in my time because we not only experience defeat but the kind of self-knowledge of defeat that rubs elbows with humiliation, deserved or undeserved, and a sense that out of that humiliation rises a dreadful inadequacy either of e.q. or i.q. That fear, that *ludophobia* or fear of losing at a game, whatever the game is… is what makes men stupid. And I am sick of losing especially when my wife wins because I have to admit that she's won, and that makes her smarter than me and the lesser partner in what, under happy circumstances, should be an equal partnership. And I am a big baby.

So, I smiled at her.

I just sat there, looking at her until she noticed me, and she shook her head.

"What are you smiling at? Are you smiling to mock me? Are you smiling to make me angry, because if you are, you are doing a good job at it. You're not going to get your copy of the puzzle back, and I'm not going to give it back to you because I've finished both mine and yours to teach you a lesson. It's like snooker. I get to keep shooting until I clear the table because you lost out on the Greek word for the sound for wind, which was the clue to fourteen down."

But I kept smiling.

She bowed her head. She wanted to concentrate on her breakfast, which was now cold because the crossword had taken so long as a result of the extended debate about the nature of happiness without giving proper examination to the question of whether *we* were happy, or *are* happy, or *could be* happy. And the longer I stared at her accomplishment, her prize, her victory, the happier I felt. And then I said the words that I truly meant and that as soon as I said them I wished she had realized how much I meant them.

"You make me happy."

She slammed her pen down on the kitchen table, got up, and walked out.

At first, it felt wonderful, that strange, almost exotic sense of elation. I felt as if the day was going to be special because somewhere inside me the sun was starting to shine and warm every inch of my being, and I didn't give a damn that she'd beaten me at the crossword or at games of the past where she proved that I was especially good at losing and she, especially good at winning.

But as the daylight began to spread, I felt the wind racing to blow the clouds away, and I could not control the overwhelming wonder of finding such joy with so little effort and so little to lose and the painful emptiness that ached deep inside me throughout the day and well into the night because she wasn't there to share that happiness with me.

The Beach

Mrs. Snell who came to walk Mutt three times a week since I became a shut-in called to me from the front hall.

"Where's my Mutt? He always comes to greet me."

I had to tell her.

She sank to her knees with the empty leash in her hand.

Mutt and I had been inseparable. When I was young so was he. He was a mixture of many breeds but looked like a border collie. We grew old together and we were fine with that.

I once lived on the other side of town. Next door, there were two girls, Debbie and Sammi who adored my dog.

They were still little when Mutt was a puppy, and I let them play together.

So, when they paid me a surprise visit, I didn't think twice about letting them take him for a play date. They were teenagers now.

As they left I said, "Don't let him run in any creeks." I knew he'd get muddy and didn't like baths.

It was March. I thought they'd know better.

They returned. The girls were in the car. Their mother, Martine, was standing on the porch with Mutt spread at her feet.

"We didn't go to a creek. We went to Wasaga Beach."

Debbie called, "Sooorrrry," out the window of the car. Sammi merely shrugged.

"Besides," said Martine, "you can get a new dog. They're still making them."

I held Mutt. His eyes were closed but his mouth was frozen in a snarl.

Breed (Nunum)

I love my dog but he won't let me have sex with my wife. We've tried locking him out. He scratches. He howls. He says my name. Really, he says it. For ten years, every night, he's been lying down between my wife and me. If I try to move him, he growls. Bares his teeth. He bit me once.

I still love my wife. I thought we'd overcome this. Then I found dog biscuits in her jewelry drawer when I was looking for a safety pin. It isn't fair. I want to divorce my dog. I can't.

I could drive him out to the country. I could leave him there. But my wife would wonder where he'd gone. She'd call the police. I thought of throwing a stick off a car ferry and tell him to go fetch. It would be dark. He'd vanish. But I'd have to explain. I couldn't live with the guilt.

At night I know the dog is dreaming. He runs his bloody little talons up and down the small of my back. It hurts when he dreams. I can't dream anymore. Not even of sex.

He knows I'm on to him. He's been watching me for weeks. He knows I might try something. Is well aware I carry the vet's telephone number in my wallet. He's seen old dogs go in and not come out.

Part of me hasn't the heart to do anything to him. He's faithful, after all. But can you really trust a creature who works sad eyes, who makes you give up parts of your dinner just so he'll leave you alone?

Maybe, he's just a shadow and I'm imagining him. That would be convenient. Like those toy invisible dogs on leashes. I'll keep walking him until he appears.

Harpy

I loved him even more for it. Coby was changing. He said he had wanted it all his life, even before we met; that he had never been what he felt he was, and now was the time. The reassignment was set for Thursday. Coby had come to the city. He wanted a new life. We met just after he arrived. We found comfort in each other. We were a mutual fresh start.

Though his mother knew I existed, though she knew her only child was living a mere two hundred miles away, she never wanted to know if he was happy or if his life with me was good. He hadn't told his mother about the operations. He said if she knew she would descend on him like a bird of prey.

I blame myself. Everyone in our circle of friends knew what was happening. One of them had an aunt in Coby's hometown. Maybe that's how word got back to his mother. Coby had warned me once that she was old-school Greek. That's all he said about her: old school Greek. Aella.

Maybe I should have gone to her to explain, to break it to her. But what would I have said? Coby hadn't spoken to his mother in fifteen years, referred to her only by her first name as if she were an acquaintance and rarely spoke of her except maybe two, three times. She never contacted him after he arrived in the city, and certainly not as long as he'd known me.

Then, out of the silence, she appeared. She had chosen the worst day to make an entrance. No phone calls. No advance-warning. Not even a buzz from our apartment lobby. Just a knock at the door.

I answered. Coby needed his rest. Aella pushed past me and saw him lying on our bed, a shadow in a room with the curtains drawn. Then she turned on me. "You monster," she shouted. "You filthy monster!"

Coby propped himself up on an elbow and rubbed his eyes. "Oh my God," he screamed as if a nightmare had sprung to life. They shouted at each other. She shouted at me. I won't repeat the things she called me. I sat down on the bed and put my arm around Coby to comfort him. He was weeping. She knew how to sink the dagger and then twist it.

I kept asking, "Why? Why?" but Aella wouldn't answer. The way he looked at her and she looked at him, I could tell there was still a raw but strong bond between them. It was like she could read his mind and stare into him in ways I never could. She ordered me to leave the room.

"I want to stay," I said, but she slammed the door.

Then the shouting stopped. When shouting stops a person ought to know that something bad is going to happen, that whatever is being said hushed tones and broken mumbling is not good.

I sat down on the living room sofa. I stared at the window. Coby and I never wanted drapes in the living room. We both loved the natural light. Our apartment was five floors up, just high enough for birds to feel safe. The place was our sanctuary in the city. We loved to see the birds land on the railings of our balcony when we put out seed for them. We rigged up a branch we'd found in the park for our birds to sit on as they looked in at us and we held our breath and tried to stay as motionless as possible not to startle them. Sometimes they were songbirds, wild canaries, creatures with incredibly beautiful voices.

Aella was singing in the bedroom. I rose and walked to the bedroom door because I thought I recognized the tune. It was one of those things a mother sings to her infant. A tender, cradle song.

I thought, "okay, it's going to be okay." I went back to the living room. A flock of yellow warblers with green mates were pecking at the feeders and flitting from the bough to the rail.

Helen shrieked like a harpy, not in the voice I heard in her wrath, but something ancient, a keening, a sound far more frightening than anything I've ever heard. The birds scattered in a flurry of feathers, spilling their seeds.

I ran to the bedroom, but Helen had already opened the door. The drapes were pushed back, and a lone warbler was fluttering in the framed daylight. The window was wide open, the screen pushed out.

And when I looked for Coby he wasn't there.

Finlandia

The forecast hadn't called for a summer thunderstorm but when one hit the TransCanada Highway the driving became treacherous. Paul's wipers couldn't keep up. Clara begged him to pull onto a side road.

"Any idea where we are?" he asked as he shut off the engine beneath an old tree with a trunk as wide as their car.

"We're beside a cemetery," Clara said, wiping the fog off the passenger side window. Their car was in a lush hollow, a rarity in the rock-gnarled area.

The ravine began to flood.

Paul tried turning over the engine but only got a grinding sound. They heard the snap as lightning struck the tree above them. The old-growth maple fell over and smashed onto the headstones. Roots like fingers of a falling body grabbed at the pelting rain.

"Being here is madness. There's no cell service," Clara said, tossing her phone onto the dashboard. "We're going to die and we don't know where we are. One sign said Chemin Finland Road and another said Suomen Tie."

The blue tore open the clouds.

The birds sang.

Paul stepped out of the car to inspect the car and the old tree.

The grave markers were in Finnish. They belonged to the hard scabble pioneers of the Shield. Paul began to hum Sibelius's "Finlandia:" "My country's skies are bluer than the ocean..." when he saw a body clenched in the exposed roots. Cadaver and tree were inseparable in their death-match for a home.

Archivist
(shortlisted Strand International FF contest)

Visitors must sign an oath not to set any fires. The reading room is always cold. The clock hammers in a minute as if it just sold another parcel of time. A reader leans forward, whispers his request. I know where everything is stored.

"I want to know about tragedy," the man in the tweed jacket says in a hush. "Sadness, loss, grief. You name it. I need to know more about it."

I look at him as if he has lost his mind. Yes, I know where it is but finding it will take time. There are no fast ways to fathom what breaks the heart but at least an archive is the last place touched by time.

Grief. Tragedy. Drama. Novels. Letters. A daily newspaper. Perhaps trade publications.?

David Hume would have a field day inside my head. Life blends so easily with printed matter. He can't possibly want it all. Memory can't unsee what is seen.

I can't forget telephone numbers, serial numbers, titles, authors, and the number on the side of the fire truck the night my home burned. It was Monday, January 29, 1977. I was five years, three months, and twenty days old.

The policeman, 5362, knelt beside me and said I was the only one who got out alive.

I brought the first of one hundred and eighty carts from the stacks but the man probably heard the sirens, or ran out of time, or hadn't time to wait for it all.

St. John's Dance

Where do angels come from? Are they born in the meadow and do they rise into the setting sun on a June evening because they do not want Heaven to leave them behind when the world loses its light or do they descend from heaven with the softness of rain before dawn? The old women of the village insist they are born in the meadows. The spirits spin and rise to glow in the final rays of sunlight before the day shatters into starlight after the sun has set. Some, in the dark, light their own paths toward heaven but despite the small buttons or radiance they emit as their circle over the tops of wildflowers, they cannot tell which way is up. If they are cupped in hands closed and ready to be vessels for prayers, their light grows dim and ceases because their struggles have led to disappointments and they have no more to give. Creatures of light must seek the light or perish. Angels are an expression of madness.

People ask favors from them. What appears to glow in the light of a setting sun are not incorporeal beings but Mayflies with fragile green wings, long bodies that appear to be trailing legs as they ascend. No one, especially the old people of the town of Baptiste, wants to admit that what they have seen is just their imaginations working overtime. Such an admission would be foolish. They would be admitting the mysteries of the universe are not mysteries at all but facts with explanations. Believing in angels keeps the elders happy and the stories they tell appeal to the children of the village and make their own, distant childhoods appear nearer than they are.

The old women ask the green insects if the luminosity of the invisible fluttering will carry a prayer to Heaven where their pleas and longings will be heard because they are afraid of what they cannot control. A June day leaves the stalks in the meadows stiff and elderly even if they are topped with new blooms, and the dancers who race from the towns and farms to their frenzy in the woods are careless with their steps and the birthplaces of angels snap beneath each step.

Be careful where you dance, the elderly remind the young. Do not step heavily in the tall grasses because it startles the angels that live among the wildflowers. If they weren't angels, what were they? But were they are really angels and what were they doing lurking in the meadows between the farms and the squat stone houses at the edges of the village?

When the sun set low over the low hillsides that danced around the boundaries of the hamlet the winged creatures would flutter upwards from the stalks that crunched underfoot at the end of June and were easily mistaken for angels. If a real angel had performed a visitation in the meadow – and angels cannot be proven to exist –

the spirit would have been dismissed as an insect. But an old woman who after her visitation went by the name Angelique, claimed to have seen a real heavenly spirit and her descriptions of what she encountered were so earnest the town believed not only the woman's words but in the existence of the small bright bodies from beyond this world. And the angel had warned her, she insisted. Be careful where you walk.

That is why dancing was forbidden in Baptiste for many years. But they could not give up the gift of being caught up in an impulse beyond their control, the frenzy of stepping and prancing to the tunes Cyril the blacksmith who could not stop chanting on his make-shift bagpipes. It was madness because angels are madness and to believe in one they had to believe in the other. And love, because that is what they call it, is madness. Love is the blind mystery of illusion that cannot be explained.

The young, especially those of the marrying age, ran into the meadow on the day after the nights began to lengthen and hung their clothing on the lower boughs of the saplings where the forest met the meadow. In the ground mist as dawn was breaking, they would wander back to Baptiste though some forgot their shirts and blouses and some left hose that hunters found during the following autumn. Those who left items of clothing behind rarely confessed to being the owners of the clothes though most of the townspeople, even though who were not caught up in the dance but were driven by its madness knew what happens in the woods. They could hear the shrieks, the cries, the moans, and they longed to be young again.

What you have heard is what the townspeople and the farmers in the valley have cobbled together as an imperfect expression of the truth because there are matters in every mystery that cannot be put to words. There is so much to tell you. Where do you want me to begin they would say and then fall silent as if the beginning of all things is silence as impenetrable as a thicket in the dark. Were they ever discovered in their mad dancing through the forest? They ask what you mean by mad. You define it. The uncontrollable drive to do something that is out of the ordinary defies the mundane conventions of how one should live one's life.

And one old woman, not the one who saw the angel, but her last surviving friend, pulls down the shoulder of her blouse and shows you a scar that tells you an oak tree, the tree of the Almighty, tried to hold her back and its twig cut into her flesh as she attempted to break free. Nature loves us too much to see our love wasted on mere passion she says and then crosses herself and mumbles a prayer under her breath.

There is so much people want to know about Baptiste. Possessions and dispossessions. The town became synonymous with the idea of mass hysteria. The falling of souls down dark wells that could easily have been filled with the tears, the drinking water that inexplicably became salty one night when one of the maidens who had encountered the angels in the meadow as the sun set on a June evening long ago, and the unanswered question of why they did not return from the woods until dawn meant the town acquired an occult aura. One maiden was found in the highest branches of an oak, naked as the sunlight and held aloft as high as the tree could reach to show the Almighty what joy and passion look like. The church claimed the town was full of a madness that drove the young to dance on that hot evening when the blacksmith's forge overflowed its embers and the sky tried to melt the lead filigree cross atop the church of St. John the Baptiste. Everyone blamed the visitation of the angel.

Pure, virginal, young girls had seen it, larger than the fluttering insects illuminated in the setting sun, spinning vertically and rising from the wildflowers where the dance made the young lose control of their feet and they trampled the fairest blossoms that could have been a bridal bouquet in the fairest season of their lives. And what had the angel told them to do? The being spun and began to dance and held out her arms to the young and old alike and begged them to join in.

The old woman looks up from her prayers and tells you that something always ruins the perfect moment within a person's grasp. Is time ever better one moment than another? People are being born. Their mothers are screaming in agony. People are dying. The Lord's kindness quiets their pleas and agonizing gasps for breath. Others are simply sitting at their tables, sharpening their knives of hulling wild strawberries the little green angels have guarded like the hearts of lovers, and having sorted the small, hard ones and the unripe green ones into a dish they will toss to the swine, realize how fragile the heart is when it can no longer control itself.

Ask Angelique when the dancing stopped. She shrugs. She had no answer. Legend has it that everyone in Baptiste still dances. Word had come down from Heaven that everyone in the town had to dance. The command came from the Blessed John the Baptiste himself and he chose the isolated town named for him as the place where dancing would become part of a person's life. Dancing, the angel said, perhaps quoting the Baptiste, would save the world and prepare for the kingdom.

And when everyone danced they felt the kingdom inside them. They felt their limbs being lifted, the bodies weightless and spinning as the glowing May flies the meadows at sunset, and he told them that when he had been in the desert he had danced. He had shed his rags and fragments of skins taken from the creatures who thirsted and died of thirst and danced so that the more he danced the less he thirsted and the locust that tasted of honey and manna came and sat upon his sweating arms and leaped into his open mouth that way prophecy leaps onto the tongue of a prophet.

The sun scorched him on the day it refused to fall from the sky until he was consumed by utter exhaustion from his dance. The long day's light licked his face. Locust fell from the sky and he gathered them up as he danced. And every year, on that day, the townspeople and the farmers in the valley must dance to celebrate the light on the one day it refuses to fall from the sky.

The angel the Baptiste sent from on high summoned the young girls and they danced into the heart of the town and the farmers at the market and the tradespeople on the cobbles joined in. They danced through the streets. Pulled by an inexplicable force, they danced all the way to the next village until they reached the sea, and everywhere they went people dropped what they were doing and danced. Mothers picked up their children and men on horses who had come to collect taxes began prancing on their mounts. And it spread. And the day lasted forever. And no one could stop though many dropped from exhaustion, some from thirst though they were given water and resumed their steps, and even those on their deathbeds rose and joined in until all the world or as much of the world as they could imagine as they danced had joined in.

You look at Angelique and ask if she ever read Plato. He speaks of dancing as the one heavenly art that could be practiced on Earth. You tell her it puts the body in balance and makes the heart and head follow where the music leads it. Plato believed that dancing was the way a persona pursued perfection in their minds and bodies, and she nods and says Plato must be very wise and that he probably danced as well. And then she tells you she never learned to read. Not even now? Now that she is old? She has the time.

No, she says, she spends every moment when she is not tending to her house, spinning in the yard as she hangs her laundry to dry or while she bakes her own bread and the heat from the oven makes her leap back as she opens the door and dances away from the loaves.

So you remind her that dancing on the feast of St. John Baptiste overtook Europe and even places beyond the continent as early as the Seventh Century, and the church tried to stop it because the will of Heaven was beyond their control and they had to kill what they could not control, and for a while, they succeeded but only until the priests heard the music and saw the crowds unable to stop as he warned the men, women, and children that their souls would be damned to eternal perdition for being possessed by the dance.

She is very knowing in a mysterious way. You feel as if you are in the presence of a mythic character and want to believe in the magic she possesses and will not reveal to you. You look at her hands. They are those of a maiden though her face is lined. She is not stooped. She moves about her tiny cottage as if she is made of a midsummer breeze wafting through the boughs of a forest and you tell her she looks far younger than her age and she smiles. Then you ask if she would mind sharing her age with you because surely there must be something in the way she lives that keeps her so vital and young, and she tells you she is nine hundred years old.

Maybe her mind is gone but there are too many details of the dance, the mystery that once possess Europe and made armies lay down their weapons and kings descend from their thrones, and merchant sailors anchor their ships even if there were no harbors in which to tie up and their men danced on the decks. They could not possibly be the same age. The world changes. But she says that they stopped believing in the dance. They stood still when the music commanded them to join in or they went too far away from where the dance began to keep in time and step with the others and they perished.

So you ask her to dance for you and she nods and picks up the front of her long skirt and begins to step, carefully at first and then more and more lightly until she seems to spin and glow in the late afternoon light the is flowing in the tiny window and casting shadows of the leaded panes on the floor. And as you marvel at her, you join her in the dance and ask, though you are breathless because you never knew you could dance the way she dances and your body aches to understand what it is doing, what the name of the dance is. And she smiles and asks why you hadn't realized before now the dance is life.

The Tapestry

I was stillborn. The day I arrived in this world, the doctor lifted me from my mother's bed and laid me in a blanket-lined box that had been set aside as my cradle. Instead of swaddling me, he wrapped me in her weaving from head to toe.

My mother was in very bad shape. I could hear the doctor telling her to hang on, to stop screaming in pain and grief, and nothing could be done for me but he would do his best for her. A woman from a neighboring farm who had been called to help kept getting in the way as the doctor moved around the bed. He yelled at her and told her to sit in the chair where my mother had draped her clothes.

My father was away in the service. At least that was the story my mother told the doctor and the neighbor. The truth was that she didn't know. They had been married, but men in my father's family had a way of wandering off, of disappearing into their desires or their fears or both.

The last time my mother had seen him, my father had told her he was off to the city to enlist as he boarded a bus. She stood in the middle of a road that few people travel and watched as the vehicle grew smaller until it shrank into a cloud of dust and evaporated behind a rise a half-mile down the way.

When my mother was finally awake and alert, the doctor said he had to leave. The neighbor woman opened her eyes, blinked, and stared out the bedroom window. She asked my mother if she needed help with the sheets but was told that they would be burned when the strength returned to her. The doctor asked if he could take me away to be looked after, but my mother answered she wanted to hold me for a while. By then I was cold. The doctor warned her that the feel of my body in her arms might frighten her, but she was not afraid. She loved me then and always had. She rocked me close to her chest and sang me "Row, Row, Row Your Boat." That is when I began to dream that everything around me was real because, as she repeated the chorus, "Life is but a dream."

She told the doctor I was hers and she would see I was properly looked after.

Her family had a plot at the crossroads along with several other families. They had intended to build a church there and had gone to the trouble of consecrating the ground for the bodies of their deceased, but the other farmers in that corner of the township were all Methodists and didn't want anything to do with Presbyterians. The church was never built. The burial grounds, as my mother described it, contained a few headstones from the last century, one or two fading white wooden crosses, a rusting wrought iron cross that one of her uncles had hand-forged for an aunt, and the lone marble tooth of a long-lost cousin whose body had been shipped home from the Great War so he could rest among his kin.

Each day my mother would tell me stories. She knew I couldn't understand a word she said.

"After all, you're too young to have any appreciation of words," but I listened intently.

I wanted to know as much as possible about who I was and who had loved who. That kind of knowledge sustains a person no matter what. As I grew older, I saw a picture of a man on her dresser. My mother picked up the frame and told me he was my daddy. He was probably off to the war although she hadn't received even a soldier's postcard from him or a single penny of his pay. Maybe he was in the city working in a munitions factory, or, she said in a whisper, he had become a spy for the Allies and was walking down a German street with his collar turned up in the rain and the brim of his fedora pulled low over his eyes to conceal his identity. The truth was, she said, she just didn't know.

Each day, my mother would rise before dawn and stand at her bedroom window and look over the snowy fields and comment on how the wind had shifted and drawn ripple lines and dunes during the night or describe how gusts had painted one side of the fence posts white.

"The world is full of magic," she said. "Come spring, I really should do something to start the crops again."

The fields have been fallow too long enough, and if the farm is going to be productive she would have to borrow money for seed, perhaps beg the use of a Massey Ferguson from one of the neighbors for a day, if they could spare their tractor, and plow at least one section raise a crop.

"I wonder what that crop would be?" she asked me, though I had no answer.

As a spring dawn rose over the far crest of the farthest fence line, she stretched and told me she had to get about her business and added that I would have to be the good boy. I always was. I was quiet and let her get to her loom.

My mother was a weaver but she never said anything as she worked. The loom was her music. I'd read a Greek myth about Philomela who'd had her tongue cut out by her sister's husband. The story told how the mute woman sat at her loom and wove her misery into a tapestry she tossed from her prison window, and how the weaving was found by a shepherd who took it to her sister Procne. My mother, as far as I knew, was the only surviving child of her family. If she had a gift there were no sisters to receive it.

The living room of the farmhouse contained the frame her great grandfather had built just like the ones he'd known in Scotland. Her grandmother and mother had sat at day after day as they wove tweed blankets like the kind I was wrapped in. I could have told her the cloth was scratchy, but then I reconsidered. I didn't want to hurt her feelings, and I didn't want her to think that her work wasn't justified and worth the time she spent on it.

'Some people write, others paint, some play the piano or compose music," she said. "Weaving is an art. Don't let anyone tell you different. It requires knowledge, tradition, and patience. It entails sitting for long stretches of time balancing on a thin bench. But each thread, each line of weft and warp, tells a story. Sometimes, when I miss your father, I rise in the middle of the night and unweave what I have done the day before. I know he won't return if I finish the tapestry I was making when he left. The other day, I walked to the end of the laneway in my boots. The ground was so muddy and almost ready to plow. A neighbor, the husband of the woman who was here the day you came into the world, stopped and asked if I'd had any word from your father and I told him no. I told him my husband would return when I was ready to finish my tapestry."

He nodded and moved on in his car. He said he was headed to town and if he heard anything he'd let me know.

The clack of the treadles began to play. I wanted to sing to the thrum. I could hear the shuttle shooting across the warp as she pulled the beater toward her and locked the weft into place. She played the loom as if she were an organist in a cathedral. The constant motion and the singing of the machine became my lullaby, and I would drift off to sleep and dream of growing up to be like my father, a wanderer in the vast world, as beads of sweat appeared on my mother's forehead and she wiped them away with an old linen cloth she kept tucked in the strings of her apron.

In our part of the county, she was known for her weaving. Most of the men wore scarves she had made. They were long enough to wrap around their necks and tuck into the tops of their barn coats, but short enough so they never trailed an arm that could get caught a thresher. I often saw women in the shawls she wove as they passed our farm on summer nights as they went for strolls in pairs or walked arm locked in arm with their husbands. They would stop, gather the shawls tightly around their throats, and stare at our house. I thought they were paying homage to my mother by stopping and saying something behind their hands, but they would move on. They never approached our door. They walked on with their heads bent as if they were searching for a thought they had dropped on the ground in front of them.

Some of the neighbors who kept sheep for slaughter would do my mother the kindness of dropping bags of wool on the porch of the house. We never heard the men approach and of the six or seven my mother knew who were shepherds we were never certain which one was the benefactor of fleece. Once or twice, there'd be a note tucked in the top of a burlap sack of freshly sheared curls and it would read, "No use sending the ram to market for its meat when its wool would go to waste."

"That was thoughtful of someone," my mother said.

By the time five or six years passed, the women no longer stopped at the end of our lane as they stretched their legs on summer nights. Their shawls must have gotten worn out with use because we never saw the women in them. By then, shawls were out of fashion. My father still had not returned from the war even though the war ended two years earlier. My mother said she was certain he had not been killed. She could feel it.

"He's going to come home," she kept telling me. "He's got a son here although he probably doesn't know it. And I won't complete my tapestry"– the work now contained a woven image of our farm, its long lane, and the rising hill behind the farthest fence – "until I know, for certain he is home for good. He has always had a wandering heart."

I wanted to ask her when I could start school. She told me she had seen an orange school bus passing along the dirt road at the end of our lane. It was full of children. She could hear them laughing and singing, some shouting. She said they looked as if they were having fun.

But I didn't want to burden my mother. By then, the mysterious bags of wool were less frequent, and instead, people left us baskets of asparagus and sometimes strawberries in the early summer and apples in the autumn. People kept their distance.

If my mother were given a gift of wool, she would first comb out the fleece between two carding combs. The prongs of the combs, she said, were very sharp and I probably shouldn't touch them. Then she would soak the wool on our front porch in a vat of her urine she saved up. The urine, she explained, would break down the fibers and soften them so they could be spun. There were once people who did nothing but stomp on raw wool in vats of rancid urine. They were fullers. Their work was to break down the bristly bits of the shearings. That is probably why our house had always had a peculiar odor to it and may have been the reason people kept away. Most people left their body water in their outhouses, and many, my mother said, were having indoor toilets installed. In a year or two, she was convinced, if everyone had indoor plumbing, urine would be hard to come by except her own. No one had saved their water for as long as she could remember.

Our pump behind the kitchen still worked. My grandfather had sunk it deep, she said, after the original well ran dry, Wash the skeins clean after fulling required lots of water. What fascinated me was how she could spin the wool into beautiful threads. She had a spinning wheel that she worked with her foot. Once she had enough thread to fill a bobbin, she would dye it.

Her hands would turn orange or blue or red and she would hold them up to me in an attempt to scare me, but she would sit down, look at me sadly and say, "Nothing scares you does it. You always have that same studying look on your face."

One day a man came up the lane. I wondered if he was my father, but when my mother saw him her shoulders sank in disappointment. He knocked on the door. She invited him in. But as the air flowed out to him, he leaned over the porch rail and was sick to his stomach. And when men from town took me away, saying she wasn't a fit mother, I wanted to cry but couldn't manage a tear. Instead, my thoughts wove together until I was certain I had become a story set to the music of my mother's loom.

Chupacabra

"You must not tell them stories like that," Fran scolded. "The children were up all night. They were terrified. Molly threw up from the terror of what you told her. They sobbed and sobbed, and you never rose to go and look at them. I had to rock them both in my arms until four a.m. just to make them settle down. Even this morning while you were still asleep when you should have been busy looking after them, they were asking me if *it* was real and *it* was going to come for them. Then they found one of the stray dogs dead, badly dead, at the end of the garden. Anything could have killed the dog. A coyote, a bear."

"Mrs. Paterson. We do not have bears in this part of Mexico, so it could not have been a bear."

"Whatever. Maybe it was run over by a tractor."

"Mrs. Paterson, I did not hear a tractor last night."

"Whatever. What would possess you to tell the children of the Chupacabra?"

Esmeralda smiled. "Mrs. Paterson, every child needs a nightmare or they would not grow up. Besides, nightmares are real. They are telling us the truth about the world."

"There is no truth in nightmares. And why should the children need a nightmare, at this age, especially? Nightmares catch up with everyone. They are the trials of the day that become the ordeals of the night. You don't really believe such creatures are real?"

"Our way of honoring life is to share our fears whether it is the Day of the Dead or the Chupacabra. I shared the Chupacabra with them because they said they'd never seen dead people.

I told them that after the Chupacabra had eaten the goats in the Sanchez' grove next door, and maybe a wild dog or two and the fence around their yard, it would come for them. I told them about its spiny arms, its long fingers with claws at the end, how its eyes glowed like light passing through jewels, and how it made the eyes of its victim's glow with the same light. That's how it finds those it wants in the dark to tear them apart. It follows the corridors of light through their eyes."

Mrs. Paterson was silent and turned to look out the dining room window onto a cluster of orange trees in the yard. The sun was casting threads of light through the trees just before it disappeared behind the ridges of the Sierra Madres.

Hiring Esmeralda had been her husband's idea. When they moved to Mexico, he had told his wife she needed leisure time, that servants, nannies were affordable. He had told her that with the time he'd be spending at the shale fields she would feel lonely in a new country. She could spend her days and even her evenings working on her novel about a family that grew up in northern Alberta. Esmeralda was supposed to be a solution to so many problems.

"Esmeralda, I can't have you telling horrible stories to the children. Cody and Molly are too young for that kind of nonsense. You have frightened them, not just last night, but night after night."

"I tell you, Mrs. Paterson, every child needs s nightmare. It makes them grow up. It makes them understand the world."

"And what do you understand about it, Esmeralda? I don't want you telling my children that life is a nightmare. I want them to believe that the world is what they make it and that it is not a box of horrors. I am afraid that you will have to seek other employment. Please pack your things tonight and leave in the morning."

Esmeralda simply nodded and began to leave the room. "How can I prove to you that every child needs a nightmare? Nightmares, after all, are simply the reality of life revealing itself before we can learn to live with the truth."

Mrs. Paterson said nothing as the nanny left.

The house was silent except for the sound of crickets outside the bedroom window. A large moth buzzed at the window screen, and finding itself frustrated, flew away into the darkness.

The children were asleep. It was their first night unbroken by dreams in weeks. But Mrs. Paterson could not sleep.

From the other end of the house, she heard a pained scream from Esmeralda's room. Putting on her gown as her husband turned on the light, she could hear the children crying and then screaming. They, too, had been awoken by the nanny's shriek. Mrs. Paterson ran the length of the corridor to the servant's room and switched on the light. A goat-footed thing with horns, the size of a wild *pero* was climbing out the window. It turned and looked at her. She realized that the children were already in the room, standing beside her. As the creature mounted the sill, it turned and smiled, and threw a glance to Esmeralda, who was lying on the floor in a pool of her own blood.

Cody hid his face in his mother's gown, but Molly approached the body on the floor, pointed, and turned to her mother.

"Do you see, Mommy? I can grow up now."

Sleep Walking

When he told them about his habit of sleepwalking when he was young, Michael's friends asked if he'd had a troubled childhood. There had to be a trigger for getting up in the middle of the night with his eyes wide-open though staring straight ahead and telling his parents he had to find the sea. His mother had caught him just in time at the top of the basement stairs.

He couldn't think of any trauma.

"Perhaps it was buried," Janet said to his friends said as they sat around a table in the pub and poured themselves glasses of draught from a jug. "Bad memories get suppressed and they express themselves in all manner of odd ways."

Janet and Michael were new together but the brevity of their relationship didn't stop him from moving in with her. He found it comforting to have someone beside him, to wake in the middle of the night and hear her breathing, sighing sometimes, and clutching the blankets to the warmth of her skin. That physical presence assured Michael he wasn't dreaming and he certainly wasn't sleepwalking.

Janet's father had been a psychologist and even though he had dropped dead in the middle of a bank when she was sixteen, she decided she knew enough about traumas and maladies to offer Michael advice on how to cope, if not cure, his bad habit. Michael assured her he hadn't done "the thing" for years. "Puberty," he said, "likely altered his brain chemistry."

Michael got up in the middle of the night to use the washroom. He was standing and going about his business and was certain he had gone back to bed when he dreamed he meant Janet in the kitchen, or at least where the kitchen should have been. But instead of the counters and cupboards, they were standing on an overgrown jungle path. The air was heavy and humid and green. Soft loamy earth felt odd beneath the soles of his feet and with every step, he was certain he was leaving footprints though when he looked at the ground beneath him there were no marks of his presence.

"What shall we do now?" Janet asked? "I came to pick flowers. There are beautiful bougainvillea just down the way, and I saw some pinkish orchids growing beside a hot volcanic stream. We are not allowed to dip our hands or feet in the stream because it is full of poisonous minerals."

"That's a shame," Michael replied. "I'm thirsty. Maybe I can drink from one of the flowers. Some flowers catch and hold the rain that falls early in the morning in a jungle. Maybe that's why they also call it a rain forest."

Janet said nothing. She took Michael by the hand and led him to the orchids.

"I want one but the stalk won't break in my hands. I want to wear an orchid in my hair and take off my clothes and feel as if I am alone with nature even if I am with you."

Michael bent down and the stalk snapped easily in his fingers. He held up the flower to Janet's head. "How shall I fasten this to your hair?" he asked.

"Oh, be careful. Be careful. Don't drop it or the clouds will swallow us," she said, pleading with him to hold onto the flower. "It is the flower of immortality, the flower of life."

As he attempted to tie two strands of her long hair around the orchid, the flower slipped from his palms and fell to the ground. Janet screamed. "Look what you have done! All the money in the world can't save us. The sky will swallow everything."

With that, the downpour began. Michael felt as if he was standing in a warm shower. Droplets of water wept from his hair to his chin and into the corners of his eyes.

Janet said, "Take off your sleep shirt and shorts. You are all wet and you will sink," and he did as she asked, and as they faced each other naked in the rain Michael had sensed the rain forest

119

was not a jungle but the backyard behind their apartment. Lights from the parking area illuminated the drops as they chased each other to the ground. Janet was in front of him, shivering in the downpour and he reached out to hold her as he realized they were both naked.

He looked at her head propped against his shoulder. He was awake, or so he thought, and he wanted to ask her what they were doing in the backyard. But Janet sighed. Her eyes were open but she was far away, deep in the abyss of a dream.

"Hold me tighter," she whispered. "He will never return now that you have lost the flower."

Sentry

My grandmother's house was always damp no matter how hot the electric fire in the hearth glowed. She lived so close to the sea I could hear the waves at night. The pillows on the bed were clammy, and if the sheets had been kept in the closet before being put on the bed, my feet felt as if they were sliding into cold water after she turned out the spare room light.

When I lost my job in the city, I came back here. I knew there was nothing here. My grandmother has been dead almost forty years. Nothing looks the same. But there was still a place for me to stay, an old coastal defense concrete pillbox that was supposed to stop the German invasion that never came. It is a shelter though it offers no other amenities. The pillbox is a useful place to hide, a defendable position, and the echo inside the walls when I speak to myself reassures me someone is listening other than the sea.

After the war, no one thought to knock it down. The pillbox became a relic, an artifact of history that soon became an eyesore. When I was a boy playing inside, I had no idea how awful it really was. Me and the other boys defended our island, whatever the cost may be, and by the time the tide went out and we could almost walk across the Channel to France the pillbox was there for us if we felt chilled and wanted to get out of the wind.

The structure remains a local landmark used mostly as a hangout for vagrants, a secluded place for lovers, and a piss bin for boys who go larking in the dunes when they should have been at school. The iron door is long gone, but the hinges still sing because someone took care to keep them oiled and almost rust-free.

The pillbox stinks now.

I went up the High Street to buy a loaf of bread and a can of beer and when I returned I saw a local banker come out followed by a boy who was no more than high school age. Both paused and looked at me, sitting in the dunes and letting the wind muss my hair. The banker looked embarrassed. I simply shrugged as he straightened his suit coat. Then he turned and shouted at me, "Bugger you!" I was concerned he was going to come after me in the same way he'd gone after that boy. The boy didn't stick around.

The banker started to disappear over the dune, but he returned. "You sod! Just try and put your money in my bank. I'll be waiting for you."

I couldn't bother telling him I didn't have any money. I'd lost it all. I had made a bad tech investment. Then my wife left me… well, not really leave. I walked out one night after telling her I was going to guard the coast.

I left but changed my mind because the train had stopped running. When I came home I found her in bed with her banker. Those bastards are everywhere. They'll screw you out of house and home all in the name of guarding your money.

But today with the boy and the banker gone, the pillbox is mine again. They didn't toss my belongings. At least they were respectable on that account.

I could sit in there forever. I could repel an invasion if need be. The problem is, as I said, there was nothing left for the taking. Nothing here. Nothing to see. Go home.

But I will wait, in any case. I am certain the next invasion is coming and am still not convinced it won't. That's a bad double negative, but everything compounds: interest, negatives. It gets into a place. It takes the best part of things away. I have a plan but no one to share it with. And what is my plan? Loose lips sink ships. Tankers are passing the coast every day. I don't want to put them in danger. I can't trust you, no matter how well you may be listening to my story. So I'm not going to tell anyone.

I spend hours looking through the gun portal. The dawns – they're always coming up like thunder over China cross the bay, or an arm trying to fit into a jacket. The French have always understood that. *La Manche*, the sleeve. I see the far coast clearly.

SENTRY

Out on the far coast the light gleams and is gone. I see poetry from my digs. It is even painted on the walls, though the meter is off and the 'it' or 'uck' rhymes are monotonous.

As a sentry I keep watch for planes, flights across the grey sea and its drowning whitecaps, like bluebirds over the White Cliffs of Dover, tomorrow just you wait and see, and the bomber noses point toward London and snarl through the anger of their engines with mad fury, though the sound of a Spitfire, a long, thin note droning against the sky still carries a tune. If you want, I will sing it for you. I'm certain no one has heard it, at least not as long as I've been standing at my post.

It's a Girl!

Charles and Charlotte Morgan are delighted to announce the birth of their daughter, Megan Antonia Esther, at St. Mary's Health Centre, the first grandchild for Cynthia Morgan and the late Cecil Morgan, and Esther and Tony Bassingthwaite. Megan will attend Anderson Street Public School until a gun incident in her fifth-grade year after which she will transfer to Saint Ursula's Girl's Academy where she will participate in drama and choir while attempting to complete her pre-secondary schooling under the supervision of Principal George Masters who will be charged with molesting Megan's best friend, Wendy Chisholm. Megan will apply for numerous colleges but will only be accepted into Rockford College because a bout of depression, possibly caused by her educational experiences, will leave her with low grades that will not permit her to enter a better post-secondary university. At Rockford College, Megan will study anthropology but will fall from a second-story window during a dorm party. Charles and Charlotte Morgan will announce further arrangements and details as they become available after a family-members-only service and ask that their privacy be respected during this difficult time. In lieu of flowers, please send donations to St. Mary's Health Centre Post-Natal Care Unit.

Roar

When men do up the top button on their shirt, the one at the collar, it is either to achieve a farm boy-look or because they are growing old and their necks are showing the crepe of hanging flesh beneath their throats. Whatever the reason, Mike wasn't himself anymore. His life, he worried, was spent as a sociopath, without showing love to a fellow creature.

Mike hated the elephants. What were they thinking? The big cats were open books. They'd snarl and swipe with the bared claws. They were designed to kill whatever bothered them. Mike could understand that. He could respect rage. But elephants were different.

Elephants came last in his hierarchy of beasts because their patience wasn't just a mask. It was a rouse. They were as capable of rage and violence as lions and tigers. Mike hated docility and he hated cute things that drew attention from his man-eaters. When they were young and supposedly naïve to cruelties of the world, elephants were stupid things. Corina, the Loxodonta acrobat, claimed Mike misread them. That's why he beat baby Mitchy with a length of iron pipe. The beating almost killed her precious pet.

By the time the circus was shutting down, Mike had become forgetful about small things such as locking cage doors when he went to have a smoke. In the housing tent, he was cornered by his cats and Mitchy, all grown up, his trunk a pendulum that pointed at the flesh hanging from Mike's neck.

The Laurel

One summer afternoon when I was ten and bored from living on a farm my father had no idea how to work, I walked into the fields. The weeds were waist-high and burnt blond in the sun. I spread myself beside our dry creek where an old willow wanted to lie down with me and remember the sound water used to make.

That's when I saw the two. He was blond. A stalk of straw stuck to his ribs. Her hair was brown and flowed behind her as she fled but she tripped on something in the weeds. Then he seized her.

She was screaming "No! No!" over the dry chirps of crickets. I heard him groan and she wept, not as if she were sad but as if a part of her was lost. When she leaped up he grabbed her around the knees and I saw the horror on her face. Her legs were turning to bark, her fingers sprouting leaves, and her torso becoming round and gnarled with knotted eyes staring at the fields.

The next day I brought my father to see the new tree. He picked a leaf from one of its branches and began chewing on it because he said it would make him wise. I heard the wind utter "O," and when I sat beneath its shade the breeze through the leaves warned me never to grow a day older.

Silences

For my twelfth birthday, my parents asked me what I wanted. I told them I wanted them to talk, not just to me, but to each other. They seemed surprised.

"Your father and I are perfectly contented with each other," my mother insisted. But I knew there was something wrong. They weren't communicating.

Other people's parents said things to each other. They'd call goodbye, argue over who let the cat out, or shout about overspending, or the dinner being cold. My parents said nothing.

The three of us sat down at the dining room table, our hands folded in front of us on the linen cloth.

"Are you going to explain?" I asked.

My father looked concerned and glanced at my mother as if to say, "Are you or I going to tell her?"

"Dear, we do communicate. We just don't use words. You've probably seen me break into a smile, or your father put his hands up to the side of his head and stomp his foot or caught me shaking my head in displeasure for no reason. We don't have to speak. We communicate telepathically. We know what the other is thinking."

"There are times," my father added, "when I can't control my thoughts, but I try to make sure they are always about your mother."

"Such a flirt," she said.

"Can't you say something to each other? Just for me?"

I went to my room. The house was silent except for the singing in my head.

Suntrap

There was one corner of the living room where the sun flooded in on winter mornings and he liked to sit and face directly into the light until he took his eyes off it and everything around him went dark.

His wife complained that if he kept pulling back the drapes the floral slipcovers would fade, and they couldn't afford new ones.

He would shrug when she said that.

He pretended he didn't care, but just before he would get up to leave his spot on the couch, or if the sun passed behind a cloud, he would bend over and smooth the fabric, patting it and drawing his hand across the surface of the printed chintz to make the damage go away.

Lately, he'd grown quiet, seeming farther and farther away from her to the point that she wondered if he heard her anymore.

Months of winter still lay ahead.

Over lunch one day he said he wanted to sit out in the garden. She replied it was freezing out and far too cold. It was January.

He insisted the flowers in the living room were ready to bloom.

He'd always been a pragmatist. Now, though, she was certain, he had drifted off into a dream world. What had remained with him were memories from long before she had met him.

He would break into poetic recitations, and although they had been married for fifty years, she had no idea his mind had stored Wordsworth's "I Wandered Lonely as a Cloud."

Odd things set him off. The daffodil poem had emerged when a friend had them in for tea and handed him a cup decorated in the yellow flowers.

A woman chasing a toddler in the supermarket had triggered a round of Tennyson's "Charge of the Light Brigade."

Everywhere they went, poetry flowed from him. He hadn't been a poet. He'd worked in a bank.

When she found him one day after the sun had gone in, his mouth drooping and one hand open in his lap, she checked to see if he was still alive then attempted to settle him with his feet up on the couch. He reached to smooth the sun from the fabric and muttered the slurred word 'spring.'

"Yes," she said. "It is springtime now. It's April at last."

He tugged at her sweater and pointed at the cushion panel beside him on the couch. She looked at the slipcover and was awestruck as the buds in the pattern bloomed just as they faded in harsh light.

Gran's Hats (Unlimited Literature)

Though she refused to believe Grandad was gone, she announced she needed a new hat. Black had never been her shade although she looked very widow-ish in her long Persian lamb coat. Most of her hats were grey or blue. We took her shopping and she found a black feathered Queen Mary and fitted with a black mesh veil.

" A person needs to dress for grief," Gran said.

She said she needed new glasses. We guessed she wanted people to see the sadness on her face, so she settled on a pair of crow-like frames. But her eyesight didn't improve.

At dinner one night we knew something was wrong. She ate only half her plate, and when she wasn't looking we turned it around and she finished the other side.

Neighbors saw her sitting and rocking on her front porch at three in the morning. She told them she was waiting for her husband to come home. He always had.

The woman next door rang to tell us Gran had fallen down the steps. It was winter. We should have seen that coming. When we got there, Gran explained she had mistaken her shadow for her husband and wanted to hold him before he flittered away again. Did we know him?

When the ambulance arrived she insisted she would not leave without her hat.

Boxes of black hats tumbled from her wardrobe. We asked which one she wanted.

"The black-feathered one!" And each was ready to fly away.

Cornfield

So if I'm as pissed as you, who's going out and find Petey in the dark? Just listen to him. Geez. Pleading, then pauses when he sobs followed by silence and the crickets chirping. It's too nice a night. I figure if the kid had any sense in his head, he'd lie down between the rows, look up through the spreading arms of the corn, and count the stars. But no.

He'll tell his Mom when she gets back. But what will she say? She'll yell. She'll tell me I'm a bum, that I couldn't look after a child and if any of you are still here she'd tell you to fuck off. I think we're just going to wait for Petey to figure his way out, maybe follow the sound of our laughter or the lights from the kitchen. Bob's right. The kid has no sense or he'd come out.

When a kid is scared shitless, let me remind you, he does stupid things. I ought not to have told him there was a dead woman in the attic who will come out in her bloody dress if he didn't get upstairs to bed. The two things, bed and the dead woman, sort of cancel each other out. Hey, if I had a dog I could send him after the boy, or maybe the dog would get lost, too and I'd have two problems – a howling dog and a screaming kid.

Maybe I want Petey to learn what it is to be afraid. Jimmy, before he drove off to bring back another forty and hasn't returned so God knows where he's gone, probably shouldn't have told him the wolves would chase him everywhere but the corn.

Jimmy was halfway through a really dirty joke and he didn't want Petey to hear so he told him to go hide in the corn. Jimmy is an asshole, but he's a bigger asshole because he's probably driven his truck into a ditch somewhere. Do you hear it between the kid's screaming, "Daddy, Daddy?" There's a horn that keeps sounding.

So what's his mother up to? Yeah, I know. She's off in the city with her girlfriends. Says she can't stand it here in the summer. Says she can't stand the heat. Can't stand the sound of the crickets all night. Always saying there's something in the corn, and there are noises in the attic, and Jimmy hears them, too. Sure, there are noises in the attic. My old man always said his Aunt Amelia ran off with a Bible salesman, that Uncle Stan said, "Good riddance to her," and she never came back.

But Petey says he sees her. The pull-down stairs to the attic are in the closet of Petey's room and he won't put his clothes or his toys in there. Not for nothing. He says she scratches at the inside of the closet door. Says he saw her once. Says she ought to have been buried in the cornfield.

The Cloud (Flash Frontier)

Our neighbor is having a rough time of it again. It happens often. He tries to shrug it off, but everyone on the street knows his predicament. It isn't fair. He's the target of something we can't explain. It only rains on his house.

This oddity of local weather has been studied by the Meteorological Service and various university climate programs.

Our basement drains back up a little. Every time it rains, however, only his house floods. It's like an ocean in there.

The water drains once the pressure of his misfortune lessens and the storm sewer empties the place.

The rest of us, even two doors down, sit in our gardens on warm, sunny days, sip beers, and tilt our heads back to feel the blessing of sunlight on our faces.

Not our neighbor though.

We all know when he is suffering. We can hear him screaming for help, the splashes, the cries to save his wife and children first.

But what can we do? A cloud has hung over him his entire life.

We'd really like to help him, but we don't know how. It's hard to watch him suffer. Maybe he'll just move away. We've told him if a house comes on the market, somewhere else in town, we'll help him load the van.

There's only so much a person can do for someone. If the sky falls on him or the earth swallows his house, we just hope he won't take us with him.

Flight (London Independent Short Story Prize finalist)

You never want to imagine the worst so you imagine the best or at least something better than the worst. My daughter asked me to imagine she could fly. It was a little game we played to pass the time and to take our minds off the smell of bleach in the hallways. I told her people don't fly.

"That's your business," she insisted. "Maybe you like the truth, but just for the sake of imagining things imagine I can fly."

So I did.

Then I asked her where she would fly too if she had the chance.

"Mexico."

"Why Mexico?" I asked.

"I've never been there."

"Do you mean the resort Mexico where the hotels have swim-up bars in the middle of the pools with grass tiki huts where you can catch some shade after you've been out in the sun too long?"

I wasn't sure what she wanted. Was she hinting at an all-inclusive? Mexico is not merely one thing, and if we were going to imagine it properly I needed more information.

"No," she said, shaking her head. "I want to see butterflies. Mostly monarchs with their orange and black wings. Do you remember when we were up on Manitoulin, at Providence Bay? We'd just walked out on the shallow sandflats of the bay, and as we came in together from as far as the lifeguard would let us go, the water up only to your knees, a butterfly lit on your arm."

"I remember that. You must have been about four. How long ago was that?"

" Only six years ago."

"Six years is a long time," I replied.

"There's no time in the mind. You told me that. Do you remember what you said? You said it had a long way to go. You told me how they fly south every year just like the birds and then after the winter they fly back again, millions of them, to feed on the milkweed pods in the ditches of Manitoulin, and when the heads break open and the fluff floats through the air like Santa Clauses they head back south again before the cold weather. They must work very hard to make it home. I want to see what that home looks like."

"Alright," I said, "Let me give it a try." She closed her eyes. "There are mountains between the desert in the center of Mexico and mountains closer to the Caribbean coast. Those mountains rise up like dragon's teeth, or at least they looked like that the first time I saw them on the road south of Monterrey. It was very dark. I could see their outline."

"So, you aren't imagining. You are remembering." She was refereeing our game.

"Ah, but there's a difference. Yes, I was there, but I am imagining you there with me, not here, not in this place, so it's different. You can imagine a real place as long as you're seeing it in a new way. Okay? So, we're there together. As the highway snakes higher and higher into the hills, the Sierras as they are called are green because the green side, the Caribbean side, catches the rain. We pull off the highway. There's a stream running through the valley. It is called an arroyo. We climb down the bank of the creek, carefully holding on to branches but watching where we put our hands. Do you know why we have to take such care? Imagine that every branch is lined with butterflies. There are millions of them, not just monarchs, but millions of yellow, blue, white, and even red butterflies. They are everywhere. I want to tell you to be careful where you tread, not to hold on to anything too tightly or to open your mouth to speak because the butterflies might fly in to get a better idea of what you are saying. We kneel beside the arroyo. We can hear the water chattering over rocks in the streams, and it is cool beside the flow. We are covered in butterflies until they lift us in the air. They are holding onto us tightly, and they won't let go because they don't want to drop us."

"Where do we go from there?" she asked as she shifted in the hospital bed and turned one cheek toward the pillow.

"Anywhere you want," I said. She fluffed the pillow around my head.

"Even as we lie here waiting for you to get well," she whispered, "we can imagine flying away. We can become angels, and I can imagine that angels never feel pain, that they never suffer because they have no bodies, take up no space, and are pure thought just like you told me."

I smiled. I had never imagined what it would be like to be without my body, but the idea of becoming a thought made me smile. I wanted her to think of me whenever this whole thing was over, perhaps lie down on a grassy hill in midsummer, stare at a clear blue sky above, and watch a pair of butterflies dance with nothing to hold them up except the perfection of their flight.

Same Time Next Year

Someone set up a makeshift Golgotha on a hill across the highway from the Three Trees Motel where Garth and I had our annual afternoon of it. Each time we parted he'd say, "Same time next year, Lizzie?"

He paid cash for the room, explaining his wife checked his credit card statements since they'd found Jesus.

Garth rolled off and stared at the ceiling as if the roof opened above him. He was staring into eternity. He wasn't breathing, just staring as if he saw something beyond the spackled hotel room ceiling and was gawking at it in awe.

I thought, "Oh, for the love of God!" What would his wife, my husband, and my kids say about this?

I kept praying, "Think straight. Think straight."

That's when the Lord spoke to me.

" Leave Garth in Vernon Park."

I dressed him and brought his car around to the motel room door. Were his shoes on the right feet? Was anyone watching?

I put on mittens from my coat pocket to avoid leaving fingerprints on his car keys, then I went back for the Gideon in the nightstand and tore out the flyleaf with the hotel name on it.

I set him up on a park bench with his arm propping his head on an estate agent's ad on the back of the long seat and opened the Bible in Garth's lap to Colossians. "Whatever you do, work at it with all your heart." Seemed right to me. He'd died as he lived.

A magnolia was blooming above the bench. The perfume was heavenly. I stood back to admire him. He was deep in his mystery.

Every year at the same time I go back there. The blossoms are amazing. Why didn't I close his eyes?

Rats with Wings

Charles was told yoga would be good for his nerves but most of the poses made his heart race.

What if he tore his yoga pants?

What if he farted. Should he look around and blame it on someone else?

What if his back seized, as it often did, and he could not exit from a Downward Dog and he'd have to walk around the rest of the day explaining he was not doing the pose for his health or looking for change that had fallen out of someone's pocket but that he was in pain?

Why didn't his chiropractor have no appointments available until late next week? He decided he would not attempt the pose, especially the Downward Dog. He had more respect for dogs than to claim he understood what they were all about.

A mystical sitar played in the background of the studio as the teacher spoke.

Why did the teacher not know that parts of Charles were ripping? How could the teacher know his pupil was failing?

Failure, Charles asserted, is personal. It is not what one shares. And why should he? No one wants that kind of lousy truth to get out. No one wants to know that his body could not pose like a dog. What would he say if he met a friend in the street on his way home?

"Hello Charles, what's new with you today?"

"The dog just wasn't in me." Would that be a suitable reply? Would the friend think he'd lost his mind? The idea of the Downward Dog made Charles anxious that there was a dog inside him, that it would be healthy to find it. He closed his eyes and saw trees and fire hydrants and wanted to go to the change room as soon as the lesson ended.

"Practice this at home," the yoga master told him.

Each day, Charles began his yoga by opening the balcony door. His yogi had told him that he should feel the animal he was assuming, embrace the pose, feel the limits of his human form, and press against them, exceed himself in both mind and body. Only then would grow. Only then would he feel the benefits of his lessons and the three hundred dollars he paid to sign up for ten sessions where he was surrounded by lithe young women whose bodies could contort and alter as if they were shapeshifters.

If Charles was self-conscious among a room of fellow practitioners of the twisted art, he felt more uncomfortable every morning as he practiced his poses. He didn't want his neighbors or the people in the opposite block of apartments to see him struggle to bend over his belly. Even with the door open, people would talk. They'd say, "There's that man contorting himself again."

But he had to have the door open. Yoga works up a sweat.

That's why he hated the seagull. The seagull watched. It not only watched, it was there every morning and tilted its head almost upside down not just to look Charles directly in the eye but to express an inquisitiveness, to express the thought non-verbally, "I have no idea what you are doing and you look really stupid doing it."

The bird perched on the railing and looked as if it was going to share Charles' secret with the world.

The first day, Charles threw a slipper at it. That was stupid. The slipper fell five floors from his apartment balcony and was run over by a lawnmower.

The second day, Charles tried to wave his arms. The bird mocked him, waving its wings back. Charles felt like an idiot.

On the third day, Charles held out a crust of bread. When the bird reached to take it, Charles pushed the gull off the railing, thinking "That'll fix him." That didn't work. The bird fell a few stories then flew back with the crust in its mouth.

Charles decided to switch to hatha yoga.

He closed the balcony door. He turned on the hot water taps in the kitchen and bathroom. He turned up the heat,

140

turned on the open oven full blast. Sweat poured down his face. The balcony door fogged. He fainted.

The apartment might have gone up in flames.

What saved Charles was the sound of the seagull slamming into the door again and again. The bird didn't want him to die. The creature wanted Charles to stay alive and be amusing.

When Charles got up the strength to open the door the next day and let the summer breeze come in and cool him as he stretched and posed, a dozen gulls gathered round to watch.

Charles knew exactly which one the ring leader was. He had gathered an audience, and the longer Charles posed and bent, the more the other birds tilted their heads and began to caw to each other. Charles motioned the bird with his index finger in the universal 'come here and say that' gesture. The bird obeyed. It was going to get a closer look and hopped over the threshold into the apartment. Charles lunged at it and grabbed it, shaking it in fury as he throttled the bird by the neck.

This, it crossed his mind, was how the Ancient Mariner screwed up. What was he doing? Had he lost in senses? He stared at the bird. It was too late. The body was limp in Charles' hands.

The other gulls set on him, pecking him, and covering him in their pin feathers until he was certain he was choking on one.

He held the limp bird and stood up, amazed.

A gracefulness flowed into every sinew of his muscles. He closed his eyes and saw a dumpster behind a supermarket and an empty parking lot where he felt he had to fight for a piece of pizza crust someone had tossed from a car window the night before. And it tasted so good, and he would fight so he didn't have to share it with the others. It was his. His pizza crust.

He realized he could balance on one foot while holding the dead gull's body aloft with one hand. The other gulls looked on. They were impressed. He lifted his leg in the Bird of Paradise pose and felt his inner light shining inside him the way a lighthouse passes its arm through a dense grey fogbank and the fish follow it thinking it must be the sun and the gulls chase the fish for a feeding frenzy and the world is in balance, mind, body, and soul.

The Little Dog Laughed

There was one day, and I don't know what got into him, but he called me into the spare bedroom upstairs and he was sitting on the floor. In his lap, he had some books, children's books, and he was weeping and reading out a nursery rhyme to me.

"Hey diddle, diddle," he said sobbing and wiping his eyes on his shirt sleeve as he stared into the pages of that child's book.

I sat down beside him on the floor and did what I could to comfort him. After that, he kept the door to that room closed. There were pictures of clowns on the walls, and a shelf full of brightly colored books. I never saw him that sad again.

Sometimes, when I knew he was feeling down, I'd do something stupid to make him laugh. I'd come into the room, pick up the first thing I could find and toss it in the air so it would come down and hit my butt. We'd laugh and laugh over dumb stuff like that. He used to say I had an infectious laugh because I'd throw back my head and roll my eyes and the more he laughed the more I would laugh. He'd cry then too, but it wasn't the same sort of crying I'd witnessed up in the closed front room.

He used to call me on hot summer nights to watch a ballgame on tv. He wasn't a fan of any particular team. He just loved the game. It would be hot as blazes in the house, hotter upstairs, because he would often say as he wiped his brow that he didn't believe in air conditioning. It made his joints ache.

The next day, we'd go out before breakfast for a game of catch in a vacant lot near the house and he'd replay the calls from the previous night, and when he'd say, "Here comes the pitch, it's a pop fly and the runners are going," I'd make a point of giving him a great catch. Sometimes, I'd even pretend there was a cut-off man and he'd have to run after it, but mostly I was good at fielding and he'd tell me how much he appreciated what I could do. He'd say I had a career in the majors waiting for me.

"My man," he'd say, "you'll be in the show in no time," and when we'd stop at the corner store for a quart of milk on the way home and the door would open and I'd feel a whiff of cool air from inside. We'd go back to his place and sit in the kitchen while he drank his coffee. He'd offer me some, but I wasn't into it, but just for offering, I'd remind him in little ways he was a good sport.

I needed to look after him. His wife had passed several years before, and he'd say, "You're all I've got. We'd better stick together."

If he were gardening, I'd hang out with him, help him dig the beds in the spring

when he put in new plants, and when he cut the grass in the cool dusks of late summer I'd make sure he hadn't missed any patches. I don't think his eyesight was good. One night, I went ahead of the mower and just in the nick of time saved a small cedar waxwing that had fallen out of its nest. If I hadn't been there, he'd likely have run over it. We looked after the hatchling until it was big enough to fly around the living room, and one day we went out into the garden together and he let the bird go from his hands. It took off and flew into the trees and we never saw it again. That was a beautiful moment, just watching it go somewhere and not look back.

The mother must have thought it was dead though after the bird had fallen from its nest and we'd rescued it, she must have sensed it was still alive because she'd be up in her tree and scold us if we sat out in the evenings on the front porch. People would walk by and call to us. They always saw us together, and they'd call, "How are you two tonight?" I could have told them I was fine. It was him I was worried about.

We had long discussions about growing old. Time is something everyone has to face. It is better understood in advance that to have it arrive as a surprise. I never felt that old. I figured it was he who was slowing down and I was just keeping his pace so he wouldn't feel bad.

"You know," he said, "the worst thing that can happen to a guy is to die alone. People leave the room during the final moments because they are afraid of what they will see. I promise you this, if it ever comes down to it and you're at the end, I'm not going to leave you alone." I felt the same way about him.

But when the ambulance came for him after he'd grabbed his chest and fallen down the stairs, after the neighbors heard me calling for help at the top of my lungs for hours, the attendants wouldn't let me go with him. The guy next door invited me over to his place, but when I went out in the morning to stretch my legs in his yard I realized the garden wasn't gated.

The old guy had shown me where just about everything was in town – the post office, the druggist, the hardware store, the corner milk place, and the hospital. There was a woman coming out of the hospital – it wasn't as big as the hospitals that ask for donations in the commercials that interrupted our baseball games – and she had a baby in her arms and her husband was pushing her in a wheelchair. I would have stopped to say hello, but I felt an urgency to find him. I sensed he was in distress, that he wanted to see me, and that he was alone and afraid. I'm not sure how I knew, but I get very strong feelings and the feelings told me to take the elevator up to his room on the third floor.

I found him in a bed behind a curtain. He was hooked up to machines that made sucking sounds and beeped. I stood beside the rails and saw his eyelids fluttered open. He knew I would come. It was almost as if he was expecting me, that he had called to me, not in words but thoughts. I wanted to tell him that I kept my part of the bargain, just as I knew he would have kept his had it been me and not him. He smiled. He was glad I was there, and I was glad that I was there too. I could feel it. It would have been terrible had he looked around and no one showed up for him. There was a plastic clip on one of his fingers, but he reached out with his hand and stroked my head, and the last words he said were, "My Mack. Good dog."

The Lesson Plan

I couldn't stand to watch her die and drag her secrets to the grave. The whole idea of extreme unction is that a person dies with a clear conscience. Hell, as I see it, is the baggage one carries. It weighs one down. It was even more hell to watch her die.

She'd always been a person with a patient disposition, someone who would put a gold star on your work, tell you how far they thought you'd go. As her former pupil, I should have simply graduated to another grade but part of me wanted to remain the star of the class. That's wrong.

Word in the community was she'd always been a good teacher. Respected. Well-liked. Giving. And she was certain he loved her. He brought her apples. He played to her pedagogical instincts.

What she taught me was difficult. So when I helped her drag the carpet to the end of her garden, quietly so the neighbors wouldn't hear us that summer night, she told me I had to be schooled in tough lessons. Love was one of them, but love failed. That's part of learning what love is.

Any body of knowledge contains what one doesn't know or want to know. That's what keeps knowledge vital, though I can't unknow what I know, and if I shared it with you it would be a burden on you the rest of your life. And even if you mastered the lesson, I don't give out gold stars.

Wallpaper

Although her real estate agent could not say exactly when the salt-box cottage had been built, Gail was certain some clues to the past of the house lay beneath the layers of wallpaper in the front room. There had once been a fireplace in the over-papered main room where she imagined people had gathered to converse, spend quiet evenings by the fire, or eat their meals at long and heavy table that had left identifiable leg marks on the wide-cut pine floorboards.

The front room, Gail decided, should be a warm cream, a hue that would show her pine antiques to their best advantage with a color that would be mild yet soothing enough on the eye that she could find comfort in the old house's front room. She wanted to restore the house. Bringing the place back to life would do it justice. The rooms needed a touch of vitality, and in restoring the house she felt she was restoring that part of her recent life that had been so troubling. Now she was on her own with no parental obligations, no one to argue with her, no one to stand in the way of what she wanted to do. Bringing back the house would be her declaration of freedom.

The room's chimney remained and she was certain the hearth lay behind sheets of plywood and planking that had been nailed in place by one of many previous owners to keep the draft out. But the wallpaper puzzled her. She pictured a crackling grate fire, the room perfumed with the scent of pine or even maple if she could find cords of that wood, adding a scent of hominess to her new environment. And beside the fireplace, seated on an overstuffed couch, her feet up on a sturdy coffee table, and a mug of tea at hand and a new book in her open palms, she would enjoy the tranquility of solitude.

But first, the wallpaper had to go. All of it. Pressing her fingers against the layers, she felt as if she was in a padded room, a place where the past had accumulated too much and had buried what was important about the house. She began by tearing strips off around the doors and windows. They came away easily. The outer layers were floral, very Twentieth century. The top layer of stripes had been applied early in the Twenty-first century, though the lines were not plumb and traced the corners followed the irregularities of the frame house as it settled beneath the weight of its own roof. That layer came off easily. It was intended to be replaced.

The large modern design of the next layer suggested it had been applied in the Sixties – the gaudy pink background, the flashes of black sprigs and leaves – was not really to her taste and by removing the first layer shredded patches of the second layer came away as if someone had torn the skin off a cardboard box.

Beneath more layers lay early Twentieth-century floribunda roses, the blooms of which were intertwined on a trellis as if a life beneath that papering fed the roots which lay beneath the baseboard. But she wasn't prepared for the next layer. Along the crown work at the top of the room, someone had applied a scroll of dolphins playing in the surf and this was puzzling because the house was too far north for pods, though near enough to the sea that a misguided squadron of the creatures might well have visited and been remembered in the decoration of the room.

But she wasn't prepared for what came next. Brown hand-stains appeared on a faded yellow print of sweetheart roses suspended in floating love knots. The small, perfect blooms were not attached to anything. They reminded her of bodies washing ashore from a wrecked ship, human shapes floating face-down in the water as if they were looking for something they had dropped to the bottom of the sea. The handprints, however, were more troubling.

She studied the palms and fingers. The fingers were thin, the palms narrow and delicate. They were not the prints of a man. Gail felt sick. Something terrible had taken place in that room and someone had left the signature of their terror on the wall.

147

They were waving at her as if someone were signaling her for help – hands that rose from the pulverizing waves as they crashed against the rocky shore on a stormy night. Splayed fingers, each reaching for a different source of salvation or, perhaps, attempting to tell her to go back or stop where she was and come no closer because danger was afoot were raised to communicate a warning.

What troubled Gail most about the handprints was their color. They had not been made by a playful child or children who, having been told the walls would be repapered decided to leave their marks for posterity to find. The palms and fingers were not blue or yellow – the colors of play – but dark brown as if they had once been bright red and had lost their brilliance as they waited like a rose pressed in the pages of someone's favorite book from long ago to be rediscovered. Around the ends of some of the fingers and thumbs were splatters and she realized that blood, if left to dry on paper or wallpaper, would turn brown over time, losing its red vitality, its power of life within the veins to animate the life that contained it.

Gail immediately overpainted the handprint layer with a mixture of water and trisodium phosphate and scored the surface and, in a matter of minutes, had scraped the layer clean. The handprints upset her. They were rising from the past with a message of despair or helplessness or terror though she couldn't decide how awful an experience had impelled their maker to leave them behind.

As the final, handprint disappeared from the wall and lay in shards on the drop cloth, Gail reached the original plaster beneath all the accumulations of color and flowers and trellises that clung like history to the room. The bare plaster was a sickly pale, indented with small pockmarks and pits. And written on the wall in a broad-leaded pencil, the kind carpenters kept for marking the lengths of wood they turned into fishing boats or an unhappy housewife might have kept long ago for wetting on the end of her tongue and jotting down a list of groceries, was a message.

"No matter how long it takes, I pray someone will find me and rescue me from the hell of a marriage where love has failed. I wait for you to find me for I fear I will kill the man I once held dear, and if it should come to that, I beg of you, do not hang me for my deeds, and let me be long gone, returned to the earth and the bosom of the Lord before anyone finds his body hidden in the flue of the hearth."

Settling Up

I went to pay a debt for my father and realized there is no such thing as luck. My father was a gambler and though my mother would scream at him and throw dishes at his head every time he came home with his pockets empty, I loved him because the worst part of gambling is the hope it holds out, the illusion that an impossible is possible, and an imagined outcome will morph into a reality. My father wasn't bad at betting on horses. He was a failed artist.

Horses were his passion. He just read them wrong. One day he pulled me out of school when my mother was away helping her sister recover from surgery, and he took me to the track. I felt ten feet tall standing beside him at the rail during the post parade. He asked me what I thought of each horse. He had five hundred dollars in his pocket and he was determined to spend it because he felt lucky that day.

"That one?" he asked, pointing to the Three horse who was struggling against its harness and prancing sideways. "He looks like he's got some life in him."

"No," I replied without taking my eyes off the ponies. "Number Three is fighting his jockey. He's not going to run somewhere. He wants to run away from something. Look at Ten. He's a different matter."

Ten had his head up and stared straight ahead. He was focused. He meant business. He had a job that day and nothing was going to get in his way. My father took ten dollars from the stack of bills he was carrying.

"Okay. I'll place ten on Ten for you, but my money is on Three. Odds are against you, old chap. Money is moving to three on the board. But it is your money. Ten is now a longshot.."

Ten had a score to settle. Maybe he disliked being counted out.

My horse won. It paid five hundred. My father bet his stack on Three and came up snake eyes.

"How did you know Ten would win?"

"I'm keeping the money for Mom so you don't get in trouble when she returns. You're out five hundred and now you're even."

"It ain't that simple, buddy," he said on the way home as he stared out the streetcar window. The next day I found the five hundred gone. My Dad had it. I confronted him about it.

"Where did you get five hundred in the first place?"

He stared into his coffee as I packed my books in my school bag.

"There's this guy. This guy at the Loggerhead. I borrowed it."

"Well, I'm going to pay it back. You're going to write me an excuse letter. Tell the teacher I had stomach cramps from swimming and you had to rescue me or you cooked something that didn't stay down. In cursive. I'll go and settle your debt for you."

"But buddy, I'm feeling lucky today."

"No," I said. "I'm going to the Loggerhead and that's the end of it."

I left him sitting at the kitchen table, pen still in hand, his undershirt hanging out of his trousers, his face waiting for a shave.

The Loggerhead didn't permit kids inside but once I got in the door I told the bartender I was Dave's son and I was there to repay the money he owed. A man in the back nodded to the bartender and motioned me down the corridor of tables. Before bars open in the morning they reek of two things: spilled beer and stale cigarettes. The smell is like a debt that won't go away.

I sat down in front of the man. He was sipping black coffee with two sugar cubes on the side of the saucer he dipped in his java and sucked on.

"So, kid, you got Dave's money for me?"

"Yes. Five hundred dollars."

"Five hundred? That's good. Let me know when your old man is going to come up with the other nine thousand."

"That bad?"

"Afraid so, kid. Look, I don't want you being dragged into this. Thank your Dad very much and tell him he's not only cut off but he owes interest. Interest is the cost of borrowing money. There's a cost to everything. Your Dad has to realize there's a cost to luck. You can't buy luck. So, head along."

As I walked along the street, streetcars passed, and as each one approached I turned to see what number they were. There were more five-o-fours than five-o-sevens, and I realized numbers mean so little. Numbers fool big betters who think they know how a race is going to go. They fool the little guy who wants a horse who's on top of the day. But there are no sure winners. There are only sure losers, except those losers who have something to prove.

I couldn't make my father's luck change because he looked for it in the wrong places, in the horses that are just out to have a good time like the boys at the Loggerhead when one of them had a big payday. The others envy those guys. They want to be like them. They want to win.

And one morning when I woke, my father wasn't there. No one knows where he is. I'd venture a bet but I've sworn off.

Winners are not out to win for betters. They're out to win for themselves, to tell everyone they're wrong, as sure of themselves as artists who keep painting or writers who keep writing when there is not an iota of success or acceptance in sight. those horses are determined to show everyone they have the stuff to triumph. There's no luck involved. Just focus.

A horse wins because it refuses to listen to other horses. It's the defiance in the face fact, and that's so rare it's always a longshot. No one should settle for less.

Pigs Can Fly

The pig lived on the next farm and never bothered anyone even though he was enormous, and we could see his rump over the rail of his muddy pen from our place. But I was surprised the day I came home early from work and found my wife hosing him down in our back yard. Streams of mud ran off his huge body, but what troubled me more than the pig's visit was that my wife was naked, standing there with the hose in one hand, a scrub brush in the other, and mud splatters on her lower legs and ankles.

"I hope I'm not interrupting anything," I said, interrupting them. I was fond of seeing my wife naked. She had a body that, despite having given birth to three children, was beautiful and motherly with a plump belly and full thighs. What I didn't like was the pig. He was, as pigs go, not pleasant to behold, and what might have been love handles on a human being seemed grotesque on him.

My wife turned, rather surprised. "You're home early."

The pig sort of shrugged and just lay there with his legs spread out underneath him. "Buster dropped by and he was all muddy."

"I can see that," I said.

"I haven't been looking after myself very well," the pig said, turning one eye toward me in a matter-of-fact way. "I needed an overhaul and your wife, good soul, offered to help me get myself together."

"I didn't want to soil my bathing suit ahead of our trip to the lake this weekend," my wife offered, and because it was Buster and because he's the only one with a view of our yard, I figured it was safe just to turn the hose on him *au naturel*, to help him out."

I should have been jealous of the pig. When we were first intimate, my wife would undress in the bathroom and enter the bedroom with the lights turned off. Later, when we were living together, she wasn't so self-conscious. We'd grown accustomed to seeing each other in the buff, but the sight of the pig next to her was unnerving. She could see it in my face. I think I was frowning and it wasn't because I was facing the afternoon sun. She could tell I wasn't happy about a pig seeing my wife naked.

"I hear you, guy," the pig said.

"I hadn't said anything."

"No," said the pig, "we pigs can sort of read moods, kinda like your dog. Fact is, I don't see any problem with it. I mean, your dog sees your wife naked all the time. It didn't cross my mind that there was anything wrong with her stripping down. After all, I'm not wearing anything, and it's probably for the better because she'd have mud and slurry stuck to her clothes rather than my bristles, and I'd hate to ask your wife to do my laundry for me."

My wife looked up from her hose and scrub brush. "I don't mind. He's a pig. He goes naked all the time."

The pig stood up and my wife bent over to rinse off his underbelly before turning the hose on her legs, first the right and then the left until the spatters of smelly mud were washed away.

"Okay," I said, "but to what do we owe the occasion of your need for a bath?"

"Well, guy," – I didn't like him calling me guy, he knew my name was Richard and he could have done Richard, Dick, Dickie, Richy, anything – "it's like this. I was lying in my pen about a month ago, get getting bigger and bigger, when I realized two things. First, the farmer who is your neighbor left his place and likely isn't coming back. I saw him load his refrigerator into a van and drive off. That was after the night when I heard his mother shrieking something about putting down a knife. He had me worried. I thought, 'yep, my time's up, and he's probably coming for me at first light with a knife.' So, I waited in my pen. I made my peace with nature and the Creator and all that, and then nothing happened. Your neighbor's truck started up in the lane, and after he pulled out onto the main road, I watched it vanish over the far hill.

Then, I thought, okay, so he's probably taking the old fridge to the dump and will be back. But he never came back."

"You haven't told me why you needed to come across the field, break down my fence, and ask my wife to turn the hose on you." By this time, my wife was toweling off, and then she picked up one of the new bath sheets I'd given her for Christmas and was heading toward Buster with the towel, having wrapped her own around her from the armpits down.

"Uh, Honey, that's our good towel. He can air dry, just like he probably always does when he's out in the rain all night."

"True," she said, and looking at the pig asked, "Are you okay with that?"

"Fine," he said. "No need to make unnecessary laundry."

"I was asking why you needed a shower."

"So, I was lying there," said the pig, "and the days started to pass and I figured your neighbor wasn't coming back. That's when I looked up at the barn. I'd been staring at the barn for years and hadn't really noticed it. Have you ever stared at something for a long time and not understood it until, wham! Something happens and you see it in a different way? I had a eureka moment."

"Pigs are extremely smart," my wife added. "I've read things online that say they have as much intelligence as human beings."

"Quite right, my dear," said Buster. "And an intelligent being has the power of reason. That's when I saw the swallows fluttering around the eaves of the barn. I watched as the swallows were picking mosquitoes and flies from the air, especially around sunset, and as the sun was setting one evening, I watched as five bats emerged from the barn. I'd never really noticed the bats before, though I'd kept an eye on the swallows because they chased the flies from my eyelids. So, there I was, covered in the mud I rolled in, and slept in, and ate in day after day, and I thought, 'There's got to be a better life than this,' and I started asking myself what I could do to make my life better. And that's when I saw the bats."

"And what did the bats tell you," I said as I looked at my wife who was starting to shiver, and I added, "You should go inside and change into something warmer." She tip-toed across the lawn and the screened kitchen door snapped shut behind her on its spring.

"Your wife is a good neighbor," the pig said.

"Yes, but you were about to tell me how you made your life better."

"Right. Reason. I know that sounds corny," said the pig, "but the mind is a terrible thing unless it is put to good use. Most pigs spend their entire lives just waiting for their deaths, but my killer had vanished. I realized I was on my own. That's the feeling people must have when they wonder about their lives, that there is no one standing over them. It is a strange but troubling feeling. And I lay there one night with all the stars spread above me, watching a shooting star every now and then race across the sky and meet its end, and I wondered why I had been made, what Creator, what force of nature deemed that I should be a pig, that I should lie in mud most of my life, and wait for death to come to me. And that's when I saw the bats in the moonlight. They didn't just fly. They cavorted. They somersaulted in the air. They ate, and I think I heard them laughing."

I was beginning to feel uneasy. Here was the enormous pig from the next farm asking important questions, questions of huge philosophical breadth, questions of the ages asked by theologians in search of God and meaning and purpose, and they were questions I couldn't answer and that frightened me every time I was confronted by them. I had grown so afraid of the big questions, there were times on a summer night when I couldn't bring myself to sit in my yard with a beer and look up because in the darkness, I saw my own death, not at the hands of a farmer with a side of bacon to take to market, but in the limitations of my own puniness. So, I kind of knew what the pig was struggling with.

"I don't have any answers," I said.

"Oh, guy, I'm not asking you for answers, because I think I've found the solution to my problem, a solution that is based on daft impossibilities, but that nonetheless is worthy of proof. I watched the bats. The bats are mammals. They can fly. So I asked them, I said 'Hey guys, you're all mammals and you can fly.' They all agreed. I asked them, 'Am I a mammal?" and they all said, 'Sure.' So it struck me that a pig could fly, if only I could find out how, and why, and then when, and where. I've got an inquisitive streak."

"I can tell," I said to the pig. "But there's a flaw in that. You and I are both mammals and you don't see me sprouting wings and taking off. I'm just not made that way."

"Sure," he said, "but have you tried? Have you ever wished for something and then made the wish come true with hard work, with perseverance, with that lovely thing you humans call ingenuity? You guys fly all the time. I watch planes going overhead. I see guys in tiny planes dusting the crops in the spring. I know you figured out a way to do it. But what motivates me even more than just wishing I could fly is that I look up at the stars. There are bears and birds and bulls up there in the heavens, but no one ever bothered to see a pig up in distant lights. I want to be the one to make my mark."

"Uh, Buster, I hate to break it to you, but pigs can't fly. They tried to prove it with deductive reasoning. They said a bat is a mammal. A bat can fly. A pig is a mammal; therefore, pigs can fly. It didn't work. In the Middle Ages someone went so far as to toss a pig off a church tower and when it didn't fly everyone said the creature was just being diffident. Maybe science works according to deductive reasoning, but not life. Life is inductive. You don't know from day to day whether things are going to add up. Why yesterday, if someone told me I'd come home in the afternoon and find my wife naked in my backyard and washing a pig who wants to fly and that I'd be having a conversation with the said pig about the nature of logic, I'd have declared that was an impossibility. That's why inductive reasoning runs life. You are the pig in my impossibility."

"I see where you are going with this," Buster said and sighed, "but the inductive aspect of reality is the reason why I think I can fly. For the past two weeks, I've had this strange sensation, a tingling, a pain, an itch in my shoulder blades."

"Could be shingles," I said. "I had those once. Have you been under a lot of stress?"

"Maybe that's what you say now, but I am certain I am about to sprout wings, and with your permission, now that I'm cleaned off, I'd like to rest here in your yard – I promise I won't eat your zucchinis or your sunflowers, and just wait for nature to take its course."

"What will I do about the mess you leave behind?"

"I'll eat it. After all, I am still a pig."

So, I went inside, watched some television, had my dinner, and waited for the sun to set. But all night, I kept going to the bedroom window at the back of the house, looking out, and watching Buster as his enormous body heaved with its heavy breaths, and the bats fluttered over the yard consuming their weight each hour in mosquitoes. I lay there in the dark, thinking, 'Well, pigs can't fly, but they can dream.' And I remembered the old saying that a person's got to dream or what's a heaven for. I guess that goes for pigs as well. Buster had, at least, worked through the theological dimensions of the question of his flight and had considered the problem from the perspective of logic. That's more than a lot of people I know do before they commit to a pursuit.

I was getting ready to leave in the morning. The sun was just coming up in a green line beyond the cornfield, and a dewy mist wove through the stocks. It was going to be a beautiful summer day. After I finished my coffee, I thought I would check on our enormous visitor. I walked slowly across the damp, glistening grass. He was still asleep, and his pink snout flared and contracted with each breath. He was snoring as well, not a human snore, but a very deep, baritone, operatic, pig snore that moved through his body and made his curly tail shake like a tiny indicator on a machine gauge. As I looked at him, it struck me that life does make beautiful creatures even when we can't see the beauty in them, and I shuddered as I thought of a truck packed with small, frightened pigs staring through the slats on their way to the slaughterhouse. And that is when I saw the bulge on his upper back, swelling, like a blister about to burst. I walked around the left side of him and there was another growing from the other shoulder.

A pinpoint of a wet feather poked through his skin, and he woke with a start.

"I'm feeling something. Richard, guy, tell me it is not a knife."

"No," I said, stepping back because I couldn't tell if my eyes were deceiving me in the half-light of the dawn. "Good, lord!" I shouted. "You are growing wings!"

I ran into the house and woke my wife.

"You've got to see this. Buster is sprouting." She sat up, looked at me as if I had lost my mind – maybe I had – as I told her to call the shop and tell them I wouldn't be in today and to come out to the yard as soon as she could.

By the time I got out there and my wife had made the call, found her bathrobe, and tied the cord around her waist. Buster was standing up, spreading a pair of broad, white wings with pink struts running along the upper edges of them. He flapped them and sprayed me with a salty liquid that got in my mouth and tasted like tears.

Buster turned his head from side to side to admire his new appendages. He flapped them until they were completely dry, and then, with his chin proudly raised in profile so the morning sun shone around his head in a halo of light, he turned to me.

"Thank you. You were right about inductive reason," he said, and pawing the ground to get a good grip on the earth he shouted, "I am going to bring a pig to the stars," and after a running start, just when he appeared to stumble over his hooves, his feet left the ground and he rose into the air. He circled above our house twice, the second time offering a salute in the form of an aviator's dipped wing and vanished into the blue sky where I always thought the idea of a flying pig might be possible when I lay in my garden and let my imagination leave the world behind.

Worth Keeping

Bermondsey Market doesn't open until six a.m. and by six-thirty most of the fortuitous finds are gone. Waiting in the dark for the last market before the Christmas break to begin is a cold affair. It feels like death as if anyone knows what death feels like.

The first vendor to spread her table full of brick-a-brack from silver spoons to old clocks that parted ways with their winding keys had a small daguerreotype of a woman holding her baby. In the half-light of a streetlamp broken by the bare branches of a tree, the image flashed from positive to negative depending on the angle of reflection. It was a Victorian image, probably dating from the 1850s. The mother and child were posed in a bed, the woman's head propped on a pillow, and the child cradled in one arm in the stance of a Madonna and child – something innocent enough at first glance. But the woman who was selling the portrait had to comment.

"Look carefully at her eyes."

The eyes of the woman were staring but it was impossible to tell at what. They were not looking at the camera. On close inspection, they weren't looking at anything, not at the child's face or even at the floor. "She's been good and dead," the vendor said. "Likely died in childbirth with that baby."

Through a magnifying glass, the outline of a wooden brace was just visible behind her temples. The woman must have been lying on the device that locked her head in place. Her hands are not holding the baby as one would with a cupped palm to support the child's cranium. One is spread upon the child's swaddling and the other is limp on the blanket of the bed. The child's eyes are closed.

160

"Her poor husband. Maybe he was the photographer. In his grief, he probably wanted something to remember her by," said the vendor. The vendor opened the back of the frame. There were two sets of curls, one brown, the other wispy and fair tied together with small knots of blue ribbon. She asked me if I wanted to hold one of the locks. I shook my head.

"It's very rare. Victorian hair jewelry and a tintype on a silver plate. I dare say there's money in the plate at today's prices if you didn't want to keep the image and just had it melted down. It would make a nice ring for your missus. Twenty quid. That's a bargain. You rarely see the eyes that clear."

No one should have to look into those eyes.

The hand that was not holding the baby was the most troubling aspect of the picture. It looked as if the photographer had just let it go and laid it gently to her side, and the delicate straight fingers appeared as if the man behind the camera would take it up again the moment the plate was exposed.

"What makes you think the photographer was her husband?" I had to ask. There was no reason to believe he was until she pointed to the cardboard backing behind the image where the locks of hair had been laid. There, three stains, as if made by tears, tinted the liner.

"They're probably salt," she said. "You can see the way the paper holds them. The marks fade around the edges. Maybe that's how grief works. It fades around the edges with time."

I asked the vendor to shut the back. I held the image beneath a magnifying glass and though the first light of day had not yet appeared, I could see by the yellow glow of the streetlamp that the woman in the picture had been weeping. The blur that is often seen in early images of sleeping babies, was not there. The eyelids did not flutter the way newborns' do when they are asleep.

"I could do fifteen quid. That's as low as I could go. You look like a discernable gentleman, someone who knows what's rare and beautiful."

But I had seen all I could stand. My breath had clouded over the glass of the frame. I felt the misery, the pain, a sense of betrayal in the darkened room. The longer I stared at the image at arm's length the more I felt the world had no right to take so much from someone, though I know death is a reality of life, that parts of who and what one is going missing with each day. Grief, though, is something one can feel. It is a shared emotion. It is the pain that cannot touch one thing. It lasts long after those who feel it have left this life.

And I could imagine the moment the image was captured. The light slowly creeping through the layers of lenses, touching the silver plate, making the sorrowful magic happen behind one, unblinking eye. Then the brass cover is placed over the lens. The world inside the camera, or perhaps even the photographer's brain, goes dark and numb, and he is alone in his thoughts and the one person he might have shared them with cannot answer him as he describes what he feels. Then he lifts a long curtain which he has placed over his head. The light that enters the room is cold and unforgiving, grey as if it has had the day sucked out of it. A voice in his mind begs him: "Make them last forever. Make this worth keeping."

Swimmer (Emerge Literary Journal)

He watched Rank bring her so close to Pigeon Point he could almost see its grey stone back through the gale.

Then the *Clara B* broke up.

Rank and Harry shouted in the water but their voices soon vanished in the wind. He wondered if his shipmates made it ashore. If they had, they'd be calling for him. He heard nothing. The current was dragging him farther out and tugging to get his slicker off.

He thought he could see the point. He could picture last June's evening with his friends, the glow of golden light on the procession to the water's edge for the blessing of the waves. The guys there in black suits, the girls in their chiffon dresses, all descended the rocky slant, careful not to scuff their polished Oxfords or let the ladies twist an ankle as they balanced in their awkward heels. Wind caught their chiffon dresses and moved the crinoline and lace like a bouquet of blossoms. Each girl, as a traditional rite of passage, took a single flower from her corsage and tossed it on the calmed bay. The sea was so still that evening, the sky cloudless. The flowers floated and bobbed, and each girl said, "I bless these waters for what they give us."

Anne had worn a yellow gown. It billowed on the wind, and as the breeze wafted it he was reminded of wild lupins that grew along the roads. He hadn't had the money to take her as his date. She had gone with a trucker's son. A few weeks later she went away to university where she met a man and became a lawyer's wife. But he could still picture her, bending to cast her bloom as the gentle waves returned it to her. She was laughing with her date by the arm. The wind mussed his hair and sent it in all directions, and he felt poor.

The next day, he signed on to Rank's boat.

"She does her job, my *Clara B*," Rank told him, adding that if he worked hard he'd someday earn a boat of his own. But the way he saw it, there was no future on the sea. Hauling traps was only a means to an end. By his calculations, three years of back-breaking at the catch would get him to the city where he could learn a trade or attend college. Ann was gone by then, but as the old folksong said, "He would surely find another."

The future could still begin. He could still make it back to shore if he knew he was swimming in the right direction. Tugging at the water, he was certain the shore was close.

He thought his foot struck a rock, something solid submerged beneath him, but when he moved it with his right toe, Harry rose to the surface, still looking at the bottom to see how far out they were.

He pushed Harry away. The cold was eating his bones. He had to give the swim everything he had. Whether the water in his face was sweet rain or sour waves, he fought to return and decided if he made it back to Pigeon Point where the girls had blessed the waters he would never leave the world again.

Sorrow (Panoplyzine)

Their lives together had been difficult – he standing in the sliver of light between the pulled drapes of a hotel room while Sadie or Sally or Sonia lay on the spreaded bed with her torso propped on one arm and one foot still touching the floor with a motion picture pose of seductiveness that would have satisfied the Hayes Act yet was erotic enough to suggest a foretaste of pleasures to come as he set his shirt over the back of a chair and smiled then snarled to imitate a hungry beast as the secretary unclipped her bra letting the straps fall down from her shoulders around her pale upper arms while at home, she, the dutiful housewife, sat on the edge of their bed in their almost antiseptic bedroom with crinoline poodles on the dresser and a mirror turned face down in its tray and wept and stared at the pale blue crucifix nailed to the wall above their curled white French Provincial double bed that was out of fashion the day they bought it and said to herself "we are done for good now," and realized her entire married life had been a foreshadowing of the hospital room with its robin's egg blue walls masked by the limp cotton drapes running sadly on their track and falling as tears fall from the weeping angels with blows not intending to hit anything but the heart or land anywhere but just to fall short of feeling real because she could not control the nurses' voices on the floor's address system and stop them from announcing a code blue for someone she had long wished to be dead, and closed her eyes, deciding it was not over now and no one could find the love she thought she had known as the afternoon sun slipped behind the darkness of the hospital annex wing, where whatever love she thought remained inside her heart was nowhere to be found and asked nothing more of her to cry for and offered her not a shred of pity or remorse as it called forth called a darkness that wrapped its veil around her and whispered in her ear that she had had enough as the sky she could barely see beyond where the other wing faded from blue to black which is the colour of sorrow when nothing but emptiness remains to cry for.

Calaveras

I felt I had to show up. The party was my idea. I couldn't let them down. I had to show up for my sixteenth birthday party even though I'm dead. My parents wanted to keep believing in me. I guess that's how they express love. They don't give up easily.

Danny's not to blame, and I don't blame his dog.

Danny is still faithful to me, he says. He has pimples, but he doesn't grieve easily.

He didn't show up for my funeral. I think he felt ashamed.

His dog ran out in the street when I opened the front door. Not that I blame the dog, although my parents did and told me under no circumstances could the dog come to my party.

The dog loves snowy days. The first snow had fallen in the night. Danny's dog chases squirrels. The driveway was so icy poochy slid into the street. Right down the slope and into the middle of the road. I think he was surprised. His paws kept working but nothing would grab.

Danny pushed me down the steps and yelled, "Okay, you go get Arnold, and don't kill yourself in the process."

But that's not what killed me.

It was the first of November. I'd painted my face like one of those Mexican skulls. I'd done a good job. I was scarry.

A car swerved to avoid hitting me and hit a tree.

I stuck my head inside the car to see if the woman was okay. She screamed. I felt my face go pale like when everyone yells "Surprise!" and your heart suddenly stops.

Winter (Uproar)

Now that I'm white-haired I don't hate my mother for naming me for the time of year I was born. She was of that generation who thought it cool to name a kid after a season. I know five Summers, three Autumns, and two Springs, although the latter get wisecracks about being loose. Winter, she insisted, was a strong boy's name.

She loved to tell me how she had slipped on a patch of black ice – the invisible glare that hides between the pebbles of asphalt, and her doctor told her to be careful and she looked at him and said she could go one better than treading lightly. By the end of the afternoon, I was born.

I'm lucky she didn't call me dusk. I met a guy by that name and he hated it. He became a father while he was still in high school and the jerks teased him by telling him had had to do this or that. If he refused they said, "Oh, but you wouldn't let your little sun down."

Names are cruel things. There was one guy I met at university whose first name was Robert and who called himself Bob. But his last name was Forpels. People would repeat his name though he pretended he didn't get the joke. When I got out into the business world, I met an investment analyst whose first name was Mayer and his last name was Wiener. You can't tell me his parents weren't playing a cruel joke on him.

My mother and I have always been close. She was a single parent. When she wanted to be affectionate she would call me Winnie when I was young, but that stopped before I got to kindergarten. I think she knew the other kids would be mean to me.

Then it was Winter, and now that I'm living my own life she calls me Winter which was always what she intended.

Was I to be cold and indifferent? Was I meant to be icy and numb to those around me? I'm not sure if she wanted me to be immune to the suffering of others or my own pain. Winter is the numb season. Just try going outside without gloves in a driving snowstorm or wiping the accumulated snow off the windshield of a car with only bare hands. Winter is the numbness that becomes pain. That's an oxymoron, but it is true.

I once fell through the ice in a pond near our farmhouse. The first thing I felt was shock. The next feeling was a thousand needles drilling into my skin. The survivors of the Titanic who'd ended up in the icy waters of the North Atlantic described the feeling. The needles were followed by a numbness that was not similar to anesthetic but closer to a kind of loveless despair, an aura about the body that says, "You are forsaken." I felt hopeless.

When a neighbor pulled me out and carried me, I'd fallen asleep. Sleep, hibernation, a dark and dreamless depth beyond this world, is also associated with winter. But I woke. I woke to the sensation of my mother rubbing my limbs. She wasn't crying. She was being patient. That's the only word for it. Patient. She gave me life once and there was a loving assurance in her that I could feel, that told me she could give me life again.

The tough part now is I can't return the favor. I never married. I dated. I can say that I've lived an interesting life. There have been storms. What winter is without storms? There have been moments when I've experienced incredible beauty, a sparkling of the fields in sunlight that makes the undulations buried beneath snow so beautiful I have been moved to tears by the sight of diamonds spreading from the fences to the tree lines. In those moments I've realized that my mother wanted me to see that wonder, that astonishment, and perhaps she knew that if she named be Frank or Tom I wouldn't see them because they weren't reaching out to me because I was part of them.

But she would never admit that. My mother is a pragmatic soul. She is honest. She says whatever is on her mind. I've asked her why she gave me my name and every time I get the same answer: "I liked it. Winter always arrives," she always explained.

"And then?"

"And then spring follows and everything blooms."

"But not Winter. Did you not see me as a source of life?"

"Winter, I held you in my arms. A person doesn't get more close to life than that." She would never come right out and tell me that winter is the time of year when a person has to take the good with the bad. Moments of incredible awe mixed with episodes of sublime frustration. An ice storm where every bough, every weed, and wire is coated in ice and shines with crystal when the sun comes out. And I know about bad weather. The spin-outs. The blizzards on the highway when my knuckles wrap around the steering wheel and they turn white with fear because visibility is down to thirty feet and I expect to hit a skidding truck or a pedestrian who stepped from his car and wandered the road in the wrong direction. Winter is about knowing how to be afraid and how to confront those fears, and even how to steer when the tired refuse to grab the road.

I was pulled over by a policeman during a ride check. He asked why I was all over the road.

"Winter," I replied.

Then he asked, "What's your name?"

"Winter," I replied.

He ordered me to step out of the car. I did, handing him my license. He didn't look at it.

"I'm winter," I said.

"No, I know what time of year it is and why you think you were reckless on the road. What's your name?"

I told him again. He put me in handcuffs and sat me in the back of his cruiser until he sorted things out.

"I can't sit here in your cruiser," I said. "My mother is dying in hospital. I'm on the way there to see her now. The doctors tell me she won't last the afternoon." I gave him the hospital number and asked him to call. I told him the name of her doctor,

"It really is a matter of life and death that I be there. Please try to understand."

He eventually decided my story checked out, that my name was my name, and that it had been given to me by a woman who loved me more than life.

170

"Get snow tires," he said and drove away.

I arrived just as she was dying on that January afternoon. As I stepped into the hospital elevator, my glasses fogged so all I could see as I walked down the corridor to her room was white, a blindness in which winter masks the truth of what it does to the world and to love. I saw the world through two panes of ice. The drug carts, the orderly wagons, the railing on the wall elderly patients clung to as they tried to exercise the bodies that had slipped into their own uncomfortable state of time that proclaims itself the winter of a person's life. I felt as if I was walking blindly toward the truth of a love that expires too soon and takes with it a person's past and the future thaws one dreams of during the months of sleep. As I entered her room, I heard her breathing and it reminded me of the stream that runs through our woodlot. Throughout January it can be heard but not seen beneath the ice.

She opened her eyes and reached out and I held her hand. She asked me to look out the window.

"Isn't it lovely? So peaceful and so silent. All you see is you." Then she sighed and closed her eyes and she loosened her grip as my eyes began to melt.

Birth (Crep and Pen)

Three drunks walked in front of a streetcar that Friday night and my wife told me she hated me. I forgave her, of course. I had to. She was having a baby, and that's never pleasant. What you see on television is a lie. In truth, there is no happy, beaming mother, naked above the white sheets, her birth sweat still clinging to her like the morning dew as she holds her infant in her arms and appears to cry tears of joy. The kid is not a newborn either. He or she is old enough to have auditioned for the part. Those are not tears of joy, at least not the ones I saw. They were tears of frustration, anger, and, of course, pain. The drunks had no business being in the middle of the streetcar tracks.

This had to be it. This was our one shot at parenthood. My wife turned to me as the baby was crowning and said so. She was adamant. The baby, we thought, was dead.

A resident came in several hours earlier. He hadn't been able to find the baby's heartbeat. He told us the child was dead. That made the pain worse. For both of us. Then the awful waiting. Waiting in those moments where there is no delineation between night and day is the worst time to wait. I told my wife to be brave. I told her things would be all right. The child would be fine. She glared at me. Her anger was beyond words. I quoted Napoleon, that the rarest form of courage was four a.m. courage. She told me to go fuck myself, not loudly, but softly, with venom in her voice. I knew she meant it. Venom is the highest form of love between two devoted people.

172

I think the baby had been the result of a very fine Valentine's Day dinner. Counting backward from mid-October suggested that. My wife and I had our first date on Valentine's Day four years earlier. The next year I proposed on Valentine's Day. It was a family tradition on my side. My father gave my mother her ring on hearts and chocolate day, and every year after he sent her a red rose. I continued that romantic ritual in my marriage. Romance has nothing to do with making a child, but it is part of the necessary pre-amble of how people come into the world. It is the chorus for a Shakespeare play. It sets the scene. As my wife waited for the drugs that didn't arrive because of the drunks, I understood that my chorus was the one in *Henry IV Part Two:* Rumor. Tongues wagging. No one knows what's going on. No one cares.

When the child finally pushed out, it was not a moment of bliss. My wife was still in pain. The pain didn't go away. It got worse. Several hours later, I went up to the natal ward. The nurse asked if I wanted to give my daughter her first bath.

Babies were bawling everywhere. They all looked like aliens, something kneaded and waiting to rise, lumps of dough about to become the future.

I wanted to see my wife and had she been there, I would have said something stupid to make her grimace with anger and smile with happiness. I'd say, "Look what you did. We'll have to work on her." And the baby, her head misshapen, her body not yet proportioned like a human being, looked very homemade. Every baby looked homemade.

The water was warm, though not too hot, and not too cold, and as I held her, her legs kicking, I kept thinking the first bath is confirmation that although things go wrong, there can be something that goes right. And after I lifted my daughter from the water and ripples became a smooth mirror with only the remains of her birth left behind, I could swear I saw my wife's reflection staring back at me and the startled, surprised life I held in the towel.

A Light Eulogy

I'm well-traveled. I've gone everywhere by bus. I've met more people that way. I'd come home with stories about women with chickens and the army in Guatemala pulling the men off the bus, except me, and the bus driving on, leaving the men behind and a woman asking me to hold her hen while she wailed. One of the soldiers on that long, muddy, poverty-stricken road between Chimaltenango and Cóban reminded me of my father, and I thought, "Fuck it all. He's following me, not as a shadow but as a presence casting shadows."

My mother said he was hard on me because he wanted me to be better than I thought I could be. He loved me. Where's the love in rage? Where's the goodness in brutality? There's no excuse for what the soldiers did. There's no excuse for what my father did, either.

Of course, my brother breaks down. He sobs. It is unnerving but moving at the same time. My turn comes. I have the notes in my hand. I stand at the lectern in the funeral chapel. The organist has just finished playing an interlude. "Nearer My God to Thee." They played that when the *Titanic* sank. My knees want to buckle beneath me but I hold on to the oak stand. There's a tasseled drapery hanging from the front of it. I want to grab it and wave it in the air and sing "She's a Grand Old Flag," just to say I got the better of my father. But I don't.

I begin. I say I had a father and now he is gone. That's obvious. He's there in his box, mercifully with the lid shut, his hands folded the way he would stand in church to pray, a gesture of reverence, his head bowed to show respect to God. He caught

174

me once looking up at the stained glass window during the Prayer of Confession. He reached over and hit me in the back of my head and dropped his chin to his chest as if to say, "This, idiot, is the way you're supposed to do it."

But instead of continuing with the eulogy, I'd written a script vetted by my mother and brother to make sure I wouldn't say anything wrong in front of everyone, I stare at the light pouring in the chapel windows. It is a warm day. The casements are tilted to let in a breeze, and birds outside are singing to the sunlight. I point to the light that plays through the windows and touches the opposite wall. The gathered turn to see what I'm looking at.

And I ask them as much as I am asking him one last time. Goodbye is not entirely appropriate to someone who is left with wounds.

"Is there a time for remembrance? Yes. Is there a time for forgiveness? Perhaps. My father believed everything he did was good. And yes, he did a lot of good for many people, but that good is the hardest thing to understand if two people cannot speak to each other in the same language, shining like the small candles they are. There's light inside us all. And what I am about to say will puzzle you. It troubles me. During my wanderings, I found myself in a dense jungle in Central America. The bus I was on broke down. I was warned not to go into the jungle by the bus driver, but I was drawn into the shadows and the darker it grew around me the more I thought about my father. All I could see were fragments of sun, high and beyond reach in the treetops. It is our light, not our darkness, that frightens us most because we lose responsibility for ourselves. I am blinded to my father's love as much as he was to mine. And that's what we must fear most. We must fear the light. And more so, we must fear the light that blinds itself."

Wax (Strands International, India)

Did I remember the path beside the lake where the maples bent over the cinder path and reminded her of a cathedral she visited in France when she was ten?

There was no path beside the lake.

"Yes," she insisted, "you were there. We walked slowly. You held my hand. Wind rustled through the leaves. You said it would rain by midafternoon and it did."

We had never been to such a place. I reminded her of the beach, the hot July sun turning sand into a frying pan in the late afternoon, and how she was afraid her water-puckered feet would blister if she walked to the cottage without her sandals.

"Did we hear the ocean?"

"All day," I said.

"Did I burn?"

"No. I put lotion on your legs. I rubbed your arms and back with it, and you went back to sleep."

"Then? Then did we walk beside the lake?"

"There was never a lake."

"But I remember the canoe, the paddle dipping in the water, the trail of silver droplets making haloes in the still surface, and how afterward we stood on the verandah of the lodge and looked up at the stars. There were so many stars."

I wanted to tell her that she could only live one life at a time in her mind.

"You are thinking of a time I was not there."

176

"But you were there when you lit a taper and touched it to the wick of the candle. You passed your finger through the flame and I was amazed it did not burn you. You told me to try it, but I was afraid. And when a moth that had gotten caught between the screen and the inner window flew free when opened the sash to let in some night air, it headed straight for the flame. It frightened me, and to calm me down you told me to make a wish."

"What did you wish for?"

"I wished that you would always be with me. We would walk along the cinder path beside the lake and listen as the wind moved through the trees."

"I wish there had been a lake."

"But there was, and I wished that if you could not be with me in that moment, that wonderful moment when I felt so alive with you holding my hand, that you would find me again, and you did."

Grains of Sand

An elderly aunt advised Bert that if he wanted to see what his bride would be like in forty years all he had to do was look at her mother. The same was true for men. They become their fathers.

Bert could still picture their first night at the resort. They had arrived exhausted from their wedding, from the long trip.

He recalled how Angela sat up suddenly and opened her eyes. Saying nothing, she brushed the sand off her legs and walked back toward the motel. Bert's arms were covered in white, powdery sand. People, he reminded himself, used to use sand to tell time. It would slip through a narrow aperture from one glass bulb to another, and when the bulb on top was empty time had passed. What the mind holds never grows old.

Bert closed his eyes but when he felt the sun was burning his back, he looked up from his beach towel and saw a woman in her Seventies. Even though she wore a large sunhat and oversized dark glasses, she was still stunningly beautiful.

Bert didn't move. The woman held his gaze for a few moments, then nodded her head toward the motel, as if to say, "Come with me."

He followed her down a long corridor of rooms, but when she turned to look back at him, all he saw was Angela, still beautiful, brushing the sand from her cheek as if Time had no meaning for her.

Ventriloquism

What doesn't come out of the mouth is the hardest part. The chortles, gasps, the word that doesn't have a context – those things are heard while waiting around a hospital bed. We thought the brain tumor had crushed her thoughts inside her head, that she'd never speak another word, and then, right out of the depth of sleep, she prayed.

That was frightening. She only partially believed, but there she was, in her final hour, not speaking to those who loved her or wanted her blessing or forgiveness but conversing with a distant masked being masked by belief, uncertainty, and faith.

Everyone at the bedside felt love for her, but no matter what was said, she wasn't hearing it. The monitor traversed her heartbeat. The systolic and diastolic numbers were dropping like the temperature outside. Winter entered her body. Rivers and streams were slowly freezing over. She was hearing something we couldn't.

About a year ago, she held a family reunion at the farm. Cousins who hadn't seen each other in years went for walks across the field to the woodlot. At the far end of her stand of maples, larches, and birches, the small creek everyone had ignored for years was still alive though ice had formed around its banks and tried to pinch the flow. The crust only made the river run faster. It was trying to say something. She stopped where she stood.

"Do you hear that?" she asked?

There was wind in the trees. The brook was speaking as if it wanted to sort itself out. A few chickadees that stayed behind for the winter were nattering in the trees. Was she hearing those voices?

"No," she said. "If you can't hear it now, you probably won't hear it later."

Everard (Grattan Street Press Anthology)

Everard is my hometown. Where the house fronts line up to face the world and the porches jut into the streets like stages on which the small dramas of promises and last kisses and cricket silences on summer nights have played.

Designed in the shape of a wheel, Everard's avenues led to a treed square where a crumbling gazebo at its hub was shelter for the town's band long ago. If anyone takes a wrong turn and finds themselves at the heart of town, they drive around the green in circles because they have somewhere else to go and do not know how to get there from here. On summer nights when the sun sinks and lights up the golden leaves of sycamores it is almost possible to believe that Everard was once the promised land. And just before the sun sinks behind the abandoned First National Savings and Loan, the rays strike the gates of the town's cemetery where I work and fill me with a vision of hopeless redemption.

When the graveyard was established by the town's stewards, the choice places were at the back. But as time passed and the sad homecomings of the bodies of men whose flesh and bones returned without their souls, their progeny moved on to better places on the coasts or the big cities where memory only lasts as long as polaroids left in sunlight.

The few who remained in Everard now fill the front rows of the cemetery and so many buried close to the gates are the bodies of friends I knew and lost. There are white tablets of soldiers. There are the discreet low bronze plaques of girls and boys who met with misfortune as they attempted to seize adulthood by the hems of graduation gowns and rented tuxedos. And there are the stones laid flat on the ground for people who spent their lives working and saving so they would have a final resting place where the grass tries to grow over their names until their stones are almost swallowed by the ground. I keep those markers trimmed. I feel I owe it to them. They gave Everard life.

For years Everard was a single-employer factory town. Most of the men on the assembly line and the women in the stenographer's pool spent their lives caught up in what the factory made — and what it made is of no consequence now because there is no longer a use for the product of their labors. They took the secrets of gears and oil and order forms and remittance slips and finally closure notices to their graves with them. I have loved this place too much to love it less now that the town is beyond Sambation.

My best friend's mother teared up when I mentioned the factory to her before she passed on. She shook her head in denial without offering a word. Everard now meets the world with decaying billboard on the side road off the highway. The sign is overgrown with sumac and scrub pine. Its center is missing and it says, "Welcome to Everard. Home of the_____."

Her son, Bobby, was a brat and my best friend. He'd been named Bobby at birth. Then his name changed and he was called Rob in the lower grades until the other kids taunted him about being a bad guy straight out of the cowboy serials we watched on the local tv station on Saturday mornings before the ball games began and our fathers chased us outside. Then he became Bob, the guy who was everyone's friend at high school but who considered me his shadow and told me I was dumb for wanting a simple life. And finally, as he was laid to rest, Robert, was the name written on the granite marker as an upright afterthought to all his names. His parents never thought he would exhaust all the variations of Robert and they never thought they would outlive him.

We both got jobs for our summer vacations courtesy of the town. Sometimes we picked up garbage from the square or slapped a coat of paint on the gazebo to appease the rot and try to resurrect the band shell's appearance where Sousa marches played on the Fourth of July. But most of the time we serviced the cemetery. Bobby would lie down on someone's grave and watch me pushing a gas mower among the headstones.

"You know," I told him, "I could really get into this."

"You're a fool. Is that all you want to do with your life?"

"Yes," I said because he didn't realize the importance of keeping the town's past sacred. I read in the *Farmer's Almanac* how Homer was blinded as a ten-year-old and taken to an island where he became the memory of the populace. People need to remember even when there's hardly anyone left who wants to know anything of the past. I could see history all around me. I could see it dying. History ought to be a living thing but all living things run their course and have to end sometime.

Everything that happened to Bobby coincided with a moment in the death of Everard. We were born in the era of grand hopes. We were going to the moon not because it was easy but because it was hard.

Bob earned high grades. He could have become anything he set his mind to. He won a scholarship to a university four hundred miles away where he studied sciences. Sciences were supposed to be the future. But then someone dropped a canister of science on a village on the other side of the world and burned the clothes off a young girl who ran screaming past a photographer. He protested the war and got tossed out of university. His parents said it was a disgrace he'd never live down.

He moved closer to home, to a college, and managed to learn a technician's trade that he took directly to the factory where he met the best-looking young woman on the assembly line. Then, the factory closed. It was a bitter day.

The Legion bugler showed up and the flag beside the front steps of the executive building was hauled down for the last time as the Legion man played the Last Post and the sky darkened and heavy rain no one expected burst out of nowhere and drenched the men from the corporate headquarters who were there to offer meaningless plaques of merit to workers who realized they had forsaken their futures for a fruitless cause.

Bob and his wife bought the grocery store, not the big box one that has been abandoned for ten years but the small one on the town square. They had enough money for a while to keep up the business but then a recession hit. The word recession means that things that are already bad are encouraged to get worse and the businesses – all except doctors and morticians – close up and go somewhere else but never leave word of where they go in case the faithful, their customers, try to follow them.

When the recession was almost over or grew so familiar we got used to it, the pills arrived. At first, Bob took them for the pain, and when the pain grew too hard to bear there were more powerful analgesics, pills that would pull a cold winter night over a person instead of a blanket, pills that destroyed a marriage in three days, and pills that could take a person past the pain to the place where they never had to wake up again. That's how Bob got his front row plot. I became his grass barber in the summer and shoveled the snow off him in the winter so he wouldn't be forgotten.

I'd shut off the mower and imagine him the way I had seen him one night when we pitched a tent in his parent's backyard. For a while, we read comics by flashlight. Bobby produced a *Playboy* he had stolen from the top shelf of the drugstore. It was supposed to be hot but we grew colder and colder even after we shivered in our sleeping bags.

Bobby fell asleep first. I watched him. His face was motionless as he lay on his back with his arms were folded. That's the way I imagine Bobby, Bob, Robert, when I walked away from filling in his grave. I promised his mother I would look after him.

For those who remained after the pills, there was hope for a few years. Young leaders appeared to take the helm. Things began to look up because we voted for them. And then the worst happened. The plague.

First, it took the healthy, then the elderly. Bob's father had been a veteran. He'd been part of what everyone called The Greatest Generation, but when the specter came to Everard, he was one of the first to die. No one cared that we were dying. We were a long way from the nearest hospital. By the time his Dad's ambulance arrived, the old man was gone.

The Legion was frightened of the specter so no one played the Last Post at his funeral. I brought a harmonica and played it while his wife stood sixty feet back and watched. She walked away before I had finished "Home on the Range." I wasn't surprised when she took ill not long after. I had watched as she kissed him goodbye in their driveway. I never heard whether she recovered or where she is buried. She probably didn't have the money for the return trip to Everard.

I tamp down the mounds in the cemetery and level the graves that are so old they have sunk. I stand well back during services for the plague victims. I am not ready to enter history yet. My job is to remember. I wear a mask. I wear a face shield and a white suit with a hood and booties. I wear rubber gloves when I handle the caskets. I burn the rubber gloves after each committal. And I walk backward out of the burial ground.

Maybe I think I am undoing time by watching everyone I have lost recede before me, but I am adamant I will not become part of the past. I will not become a front porch or a crumbling bandshell. The future is what I cannot see behind me.

It may be dangerous to walk backward but I know every inch of ground in the graveyard and I know wherever I go within its bounds I will not fall into an open grave. But just in case I should, I carry a shovel with me on so I can dig my way out. It is a yellow shovel. I wear an orange workman's vest, a green hard hat, and a red plaid shirt hanging over top of my blue jeans. Caution comes in many colors and I always stop and marvel when a rainbow forms over the town and frames the graveyard.

Rainbows are a sign from God or a postcard from Bobby promising terrible things won't happen again to Everard. And I will keep backing away from everything I have known until I have backed away far enough to say, "That was the past. Now show me the future."

The future insists I'm a blind boy, a walking, talking encyclopedia of the town's story. I tell the future I am not blind but just a hostage here. I saw what the future was doing to us all. The future says it will make amends.

When I am ready to see what lies ahead I am certain it will be so enormous, so complex, and astounding I will wish I had another life to take it all in not as what has been but as what will be. And I will follow the rainbow over Everard to see where it ends.

Hyla Smiles

I collect old cameras at flea markets, so I set aside some of my days in Paris to search them out.

I bought a pricey Duarté. The film was still inside, and someone feared it might open, so they tied it shut with string piercing a cardboard a note that read "Le derrière été de Hyla, Juillet 40."

Once home, I went to my darkroom and carefully developed the brittle film. The emulsion still held its image in the hidden silver, and I sat down and wept as the prints emerged from their chemical bath.

A young woman is smiling and sitting on a wall beside the Seine.

She points at something that has startled her beyond the image's frame and with the other hand, she shades her eyes from the light so we cannot see into the future.

Literary Awards

Shortlisted, Edinburgh Flash Fiction Prize, Winter 2022

Shortlisted, Strands International Fiction Prize, "Archivist," Autumn, 2021

Shortlisted, Strands International Fiction Prize, "The Langlois Bridge, Autumn 2021

Shortlisted, Carter V. Cooper Prize, Exile Editions, Toronto, 2021

Shortlisted, *Strand International Fiction Prize,* Mumbai, 2021

Lynn Fraser Fiction Prize, "Pas de Deux," *Freefall Magazine,* Calgary, Alberta, September 2021.

Winner, Libretto Poetry Chapbook Prize, "Telling the Bees," Nigeria, 2020

Strand International Fiction Prize (third), Mumbai, India, 2021

London Independent Fiction Prize (finalist) (UK), 2021

Shortlisted Fish Fiction Prize, (third), "Walnut," Ireland, 2020

Freefall Prize for Poetry (winner), 2020

Shortlisted, Fish Flash Fiction Prize, "A Short Film about Seagulls," 2020

Bridport Prize for Flash Fiction, "A Short Film About Seagulls," 2020 (longlisted)

Montreal International Poetry Prize (shortlisted), 2020

Guernsey Poetry Prize (4 Runner up placings), 2020

Bath Short Fiction Prize, (UK), 2020

Pushcart Prize Nomination, from Nunum, "Leash," Winter 2020.

Pushcart Prize Nomination from The Hong Kong Review, "The Ghosts," Winter 2020

Anton Chekhov Prize for Fiction, (UK), 2019 (winner)
Bridport Prize for Poetry (UK), (shortlist), 2019
Retreat West Fiction Prize, (UK) (second), 2019
Short-listed, Tom Gallon Award for Fiction (London, Society of
    Authors, 2019)
Fish, Flash Fiction Prize (Ireland), double-long list, 2019
National Poetry Prize (UK), short-list 2019
London Independent Short Story Prize, double shortlist, 2018
Fish Publishing Poetry Prize (Ireland), shortlist and longlist, 2018
Carter V. Cooper Fiction Prize, Long list, 2018
Gwendolyn MacEwen Prize for Poetry, Long list, 2018
Bridport Prize for Fiction, longlist, 2018
The Woolf Poetry Prize, Winner, 2018
Freefall Poetry Prize, Third Place, 2018
Gregory O'Donoghue Prize for Poetry, Honorable Mention,
    2018
Montreal International Poetry Prize, Shortlist, 2017
Raymond Souster Prize, Finalist, 2016
Short-listed, Carter V. Cooper Fiction Prize, 2016
Montreal International Poetry Prize, Shortlist, 2015
MacEwen Prize for Poetry (Exile Editions), winner best single
    poem, 2015, 2016
Barrie Arts Award Excellence in the Arts, Lifetime Achievement
    Award, 2015
Fred Cogswell Prize (Third Place) for best book of poems in
    Canada (2015)
Winner, Indie Fab Award Finalist (for the best book of poems
    published in North America for The Independent Booksellers
    Association of America, 2015
Winner, IP Medal, Independent Publishers Association of
    America, (for *The Seasons*), 2015
Short-listed, Carter V. Cooper Short Fiction Prize (for "Tilting"),
    2015
Third Prize, *Freefall Magazine* National Poetry Prize (for "The
    Thin Man"), 2015
Ontario Arts Council Works-in-Progress Grant, 2011
Top Ten, Finalist. TV Ontario Best Lecturer Competition, 2010
Finalist, James Hearst Memorial Prize, 2010

Finalist, Margaret Reid Formal Poetry Prize, August 2006
Finalist, Bridport Prize, UK, March 2006
Ontario Arts Council Works-in-Progress Grant, May 2005
Runner-Up, Word Press Prize, Cincinnati, Ohio, 2004 for *Oceans*
Honorable Mention, T.S. Eliot Poetry Prize, 2000 (for *Anywhere)*
Ruth Cable Memorial Prize for Poetry, 1998
Finalist, Gerald Lampert Award, 1989 (for *The Open Room*)
E.J. Pratt Gold Medal and Prize for Poetry, 1980
E.J. Pratt Gold Medal and Prize for Poetry, 1981
Alta Lind Cook Award, 1981,
Alta Lind Cook Award, 1982
Ontario Graduate Scholarship, 1986
SSHRC Graduate Scholarship, 1987, 1988
McMaster University Graduate Fellowship, 1986, 1987, 1988
McMaster University Travel Fellowships, 1987, 1988
SSHRC Doctoral Fellowship, 1987, 1988
Runner-Up, Gerald Lampert Award, 1989
SSHRCC Post-Doctoral Fellowship, 1988-1990
School of Continuing Studies Excellence in Teaching Award, 1996
Lifetime Pass, National Baseball Hall of Fame, Cooperstown, New York
Ontario Arts Council Writers Reserve Grants, 1987, 1988, 1990, 1992, 1993, 1994, 1995, 2002, 2003, 2005, 2007, 2008, 2009, 2010, 2011, 2012, 2013, 2014, 2015, 2016, 2017, 2018, 2019, 2020, 2021

About the Author

Bruce Meyer is the author of sixty-eight books of poetry, short stories, flash fiction, and literary non-fiction. His most recent collections of poems are *McLuhan's Canary* (Guernica Editions, 2019), *The First Taste: New and Selected Poems* (Black Moss Press, 2018), *Telling the Bees* (Libretto Press Nigeria, 2020), and *Grace of Falling Stars* (Black Moss, 2021). His most recent collections of short fiction are *A Feast of Brief Hopes* (Guernica Editions, 2018), *Down in the Ground* (Guernica Editions, 2020), *The Hours: Stories from a Pandemic* (Ace of Swords, 2021), and *Toast Soldiers* (Crowsnest Books, 2021). His poems and stories have won or been shortlisted for numerous international prizes. He was the inaugural Poet Laureate of the City of Barrie from 2010 to 2014. He teaches at Georgian College and lives in Barrie, Ontario with his wife Kerry, their daughter Katie, and their dog, Daisy.

Acknowledgments

Some of the stories in this book have appeared previously in the following magazines, and the author is grateful to the editors and staff for their hard work and warm reception of the short stories in this book.

"Wheel" (*Fictive Dream*); "Cuba" (*Retreat West* Short Story Prize, shortlist);; "Toothbrush" (*Hash Journal*); "Rust" (London Independent Short Story Prize, shortlist); "The Trailer" (London Independent Short Story Prize, shortlist),; "Aces" (*Wingless Dreamer* and *Wild World*); "The Boiling Point" (*A Chronicle of Magpies*, Tightrope Books); "The Old Man" (*Strands International* Short Story Prize, shortlist); "Archivist" (*Strands International* Short Story Prize, shortlist); "Swimmer" (*Emerge*); "A Light Eulogy" (*Bangalore Review*); "Ventriloquism" (*Release the Words*); "Everard" (*Grattan Street Press*); "Wax" (*Strands International*); "The Cloud" (*Flash Frontiers*); "The Little Dog Laughed" (*Bacopa Review & The Blanket Sea*); "Same Time Next Year" (*Free Spirit*); "Flight" (London Independent Short Story Prize, shortlisted); "Birth" (*Fictive Dream*); "Arums" (*Lothlorian Review & Crèpe and Pen*); "Winter" (*Uproar*); "Rare Flower" (*Fiction North*); "A Short Film about Seagulls" (Bridport Flash Fiction Prize, shortlisted); "It's a Girl" (*Nunum*, Nomintated for a Pushcart Prize); "Chupacabra" (formerly 'Corridor of Light Through a Jewel, *Fictive Review*); "Happy" (*Finding the Birds*); "Sorrow" (*Panoplyzine*); "Gran's Hats" (*Unlimited Literature*); "Afternoon" (*Heartwood Literary Journal*); "Urineworts" '(Winner, Anton Chekhov Prize, *New Flash Fiction*);

"Rats with Wings" (*Thirty West*); How to Draw a Frog (shortlisted, Edinburgh Flash Fiction Prize); The Langlois Bridge (shortlisted, *Strands International* Short Fiction Prize).

The author wishes to thank Marty Gervais, Laura Black, and Howard Aster of Mosaic Press for their kindness and generous support of these flash fictions. The author also expresses his gratitude to Kerry Johnston, Katie Meyer, Margaret Meyer, and Dr. Carolyn Meyer for their kindness and belief in his writing.